The Devil's Ladder

Graham Joyce is the author of nine adult novels and has won numerous awards for his writing, including four British Fantasy Awards and the 2003 World Fantasy Award for *The Facts of Life*. He teaches creative writing at Nottingham Trent University and lives in Leicester with his wife and two children. *The Devil's Ladder* is his fourth children's novel published by Faber

Praise for *Three ways to Snog an Alien*:

'Many of Graham Joyce's novels for adults explore the grey zone where fantasy and reality overlap, and *Three ways to Snog an Alien* pulls off the same trick wittily, with a touching sense of humour. The mystery – girls are not of this earth – is sustained throughout the book, its comic and dramatic potential fully exploited, and the pivotal mystery is left, rightly, unresolved.' *Financial Times*

Praise for *TWOC*:

'The characters are strong, the deliciou▮ ▮rose draws you in and Joyce cunningly keeps b▮ ▮little bits of info so that you just have to keep r▮ ▮ling.' *SFX Magazine*

'A terrific teen novel, *TWOC* [is] sharply o▮ ▮ved.' *TES Scotland*

'I can't think of a bad word to say about it . . ▮ ▮WOC is a gripping book . . . The story has action, h▮ ▮our, sorrow and one of the best plot twists I am eve▮ ▮kely to read . . . *TWOC* will appeal to any teenager.' *Leicester Mercury*

Praise for *Do the Creepy Thing*:

'A compelling, thought-provoking read, undoubtedly creepy but also ultimately an affirmation of the power of integrity . . . A terrific teen novel.' *Guardian*

'This is a tightly written novel with pace and plenty of action, well structured suspense and a satisfying conclusion that avoids the obvious.' *Carousel*

The Devil's Ladder

GRAHAM JOYCE

faber and faber

First published in 2009
by Faber and Faber Limited
Bloomsbury House, 74–77 Great Russell Street,
London WC1B 3DA

Typeset by Faber and Faber Limited
Printed in England by CPI Bookmarque, Croydon

The right of Graham Joyce to be identified as author of this
work has been asserted in accordance with Section 77 of the
Copyright, Designs and Patents Act 1988

A CIP record for this book
is available from the British Library

ISBN 978–0–571–24247–4

2 4 6 8 10 9 7 5 3 1

To Joseph

1

Someone had written something on the wall.

What they'd written on the wall shouldn't really matter, even though it later proved to change Sophie's life. But when Sophie saw what was daubed there in white paint and letters three feet high, she had to stop dead in her tracks.

Sophie had seen the message before. She'd seen it in a dream.

That was only the first strange thing to happen that morning. The second was that she was bumped in the back by the Geek. He'd been walking immediately behind her with his nose in a book and when she'd stopped dead he walked straight into her and dropped his book.

'You don't just stop in front of people!' the Geek said fiercely, bobbing down to recover his book. He had wild floppy hair and it fell across his eyes as he rescued his book from the wet pavement.

Sophie was taken aback. Her mind was still on

1

the writing on the wall. 'Well, you should watch where you're going!'

Sophie had seen the Geek walking to school with his nose in a book every morning for almost two years now but rarely took much notice of him. He walked the same way to school as she did: down the long, straight, tree-lined Parkland Drive; over the little footbridge by the washbrook; by the derelict red-brick farmhouse with its lopsided demolition notices; alongside the church of Mary Magdalene; past the children's playground where the junkies dealt in drugs after nightfall; and over the traffic lights to Mill Street. They'd walked the same way, within minutes of each other, every school day for two years and had never spoken a word. Until today.

Maybe it wasn't so odd that they hadn't spoken, since they didn't go to the same school. Sophie went to the all-girls state school Sir Abraham South, while the Geek, in his claret blazer, went to the private fee-paying Leicester Castle Grammar School for Boys. The two schools just happened to be built within a few hundred yards of each other, and might have led to some pleasant mixing between the girls of Abby South and the boys of Castle, as they were known in shorthand, but they might just as well have been built on different planets. The boys from Castle Gate looked down on their state-school neighbours, regarding the girls as rough and ignorant. Meanwhile the girls from Abby South saw the Castle boys as stuck-up snobs, wimps who were permanently ripe for teasing.

When they could be bothered to tease them, that is. Which wasn't very often. And that's why someone like the Geek could walk the same route as Sophie to school every day with never a word. Anyway, the Geek had his own tormentors. Sophie had noticed that on more than one occasion the Geek had had a book torn out his hands by the same knot of bullying boys. More than once she'd felt sorry for him as he stood and waited patiently as his book was tossed about over his head. Usually it landed on the floor as his tormentors ran away guffawing at their own brilliance. He would quietly pick up the book from the pavement, find his page, stick his nose between the covers and carry on walking.

Sophie was about to add that what the Geek did was actually dangerous. Walking the streets with your head in a book could lead to all kinds of accidents. But as she opened her mouth to speak she was stopped dead for the second time that morning. It was the title of the book that had stunned her.

'What?' said the Geek. 'What are you staring at?'

'Nothing,' Sophie mumbled.

3

The Geek scowled at her, quickly found his place in his book and walked on, still reading.

The title of the Geek's book was *The Time Has Come.*

Sophie was close enough to school to hear the first bell. She needed to hurry if she didn't want to be late. She hitched her rucksack on her back and took one last look at the graffiti scrawled in white paint on the red bricks.

It said, simply, THE TIME HAS COME

Three things, and she couldn't stop thinking about them. English, Maths, French, Science, PE, History all fell around her ears from the tree of knowledge with as much impact as an autumn leaf. Even her best friends, Amy and Suki, said that she was like someone in a trance. And in a way she was, thinking about those three things.

One was the dream. The second thing was the writing on the wall, which was exactly as it had been in her dream. And the third was the title of the Geek's book, repeating what had been written on the wall, which was of course repeating what had been in her dream.

Trying to figure out what it all meant was driving Sophie crazy.

'Did you hear what I said? You're fifteen hundred

miles away!' It was Amy, shovelling her books into her bag. 'The bell just went!'

It was true. The bell to end the last lesson of the school day had just sounded dimly for Sophie. 'What?'

'What? What?' Amy cupped her hand to her mouth like a megaphone. 'Helloooooooooo! Anyone at home in Sophie's fat head?'

'What did you say?'

'I said Suki found a great place to hang out. She went last week and said it was pretty cool. I thought I might give it a try.'

Suki joined them. She was a pretty half-Malaysian girl with glossy hair swept up in a pony-tail. 'Want to come with us?'

'Where is it?'

'Duh!' went Amy, sticking out her tongue. 'I just told you. Come and find out, straight after school.'

Sophie thought about it. She wouldn't have minded joining them, and if she didn't tag along with Amy and Suki she'd start to feel left out of things. But there was something else she just had to do.

'I can't right now. Next time.'

'Okay,' Amy said, already turning away.

But Suki folded her arms and squinted at Sophie. 'What you doing that you can't come with us?'

'Just stuff,' Sophie said. She pretended to be absorbed with packing her pens and pencils into the shiny pink pencil case Amy had bought her as a gift from her last holiday in Devon.

'Stuff,' went Suki. She cocked her head to one side. 'Not a *boy* by any chance, is it?'

'What boy?' Amy said, suddenly interested again.

'Oh, you're sharp as a whip, Suki,' said Sophie. 'You catch me out every time. Actually there are several of them. All big admirers of mine, you know.'

Suki lost interest, and so did Amy. None of them had – or had ever had – a proper boyfriend. But they did seem to spend rather a lot of time talking about boys lately.

Suki was Sophie's longest-standing friend. They'd done a lot of stuff together, going back to sleep-overs when they were just kids. They gone through a spell where they'd borrowed each other's clothes, texted each other constantly and lived in each other's pockets. They'd grown out of that phase, but the friendship was still strong. Once they went on a double-date with a couple of boys, and it had turned out to be a disaster when Sophie broke a stupid heel she was wearing and fell over. Suki had stuck with Sophie, abandoning the boys and howl-ing and cackling like witches at their efforts. Suki

6

was fun and she was loyal. Her only downside was that she demanded a fierce loyalty back in return, and whenever Sophie wanted to go her own way, Suki could sometimes take it as a slight.

Sophie said goodbye to her two friends and hurried out of the classroom. She was on a mission. But she had to admit that Suki really was a smart cookie. She had an intuition like a heat-seeking missile. Because Sophie really was going after a boy. She had to intercept the Geek on his way home.

The strange string of events from that morning was burning her up. It was like she'd carried a strange mist back with her from her dream and it was still hanging around her. She hadn't been able to think about anything else all day. She had to intercept the Geek and get him to tell her what was in that book.

Sophie sped along the corridors, burst through the doors and hurried along the school yard. The driveway was thronged with girls in their black school uniforms. She had to skip smartly between the lines of girls to get past them. The boys' school finished a few minutes earlier than Abby South, but she knew that if she hurried she'd have a chance of catching the Geek as he made his slow way home.

As she dashed out between the school gates someone called her, but she just waved and ignored them. Turning onto Abercombie Road she hurried along, wishing her bag wasn't so heavy. When she came abreast of the red brick wall that had triggered this morning's small accident with the Geek, she glanced up at the writing.

She had to stop dead for the second time that day. There wasn't any writing. That is to say the graffiti, the slogan that had been painted there, was gone. Completely disappeared. There wasn't even the faintest outline of the huge white letters that had been there this morning. Either the slogan had been scrubbed away or it was never there in the first place. There was no writing on the wall.

I'm going mad, thought Sophie.

Then she spotted the Geek, about a hundred yards ahead of her. As ever he had his nose in a book: presumably the book he'd dropped that morning when he'd collided with her.

Sophie set off after him.

The Geek had already reached the traffic lights on the busy Milford Road before she caught up with him. She saw him press the crossing button without even looking up from his book. Still without looking up, when the lights changed he crossed the road. By the time Sophie reached the lights, they had changed and she had to wait for the traffic to roar past. She watched the Geek swing right and head down towards the church of Mary Magdalene and the derelict farmhouse near the washbrook.

She crept up behind him, wondering how to approach him. She couldn't just come right out and demand to see the book he was reading. The Geek was a dawdler, so it was easy to keep pace with him and overtake him.

She pretended to do a double-take as she walked ahead of him. 'Oh it's you,' Sophie said. 'Look, I'm sorry about this morning. It was my fault.'

The Geek stopped dead. 'What?'

'This morning. When you bumped into me. My fault.'

'What?' He looked to right and left, as if sensing this was a trap. He lifted a hand from his book and stroked it through his long mop of chestnut curls.

'I just thought I'd say sorry.'

'What?'

'Heck, is that all you say?'

The Geek opened his mouth as if to say *what* again, but changed his mind. He looked at Sophie, his eyes huge behind the clear glass of his spectacles. He looked again at the playground to his left and to the church graveyard on his right, as if a gang of enemies might jump out on him at any moment.

Sophie tried again. 'I just thought I'd apologise

for this morning, that's all.'

'Oh. Okay,' said the Geek. With that he turned and continued on his way.

Sophie stood with her hands on her hips, wondering what to do next. She just had to take a look at his book. She caught up with him a second time, but before she had a chance to speak, the Geek made a little groan.

Now Sophie saw why he'd been looking round him, checking out the nearby playground and the graveyard. Three slightly older boys stepped out from behind the bushes into the path in front of them.

'Hey,' said one of the boys, a burly ginger with close-cropped hair and wild freckles. 'If it isn't our old friend the Geek!'

A second boy, short and squat with a pug nose, said, 'Hey, geeky! What's this, found yourself a girl-friend?'

The third boy was smoking a cigarette. His white shirt hung outside his trousers. He just snorted.

They all came over to where Sophie and the Geek were standing.

'Are you his girlfriend?' the ginger said to Sophie. He leaned in towards her, letting his tongue hang out of his mouth.

'Maybe I am, maybe I'm not,' said Sophie.

'What's it to you?'

'Oooo, hard case, incha?'

'Watch out,' said the pug-nosed one. 'She's from Abby. She'll bite you.'

'No,' Sophie said, 'you don't look at all appetising. In fact you look a bit . . . *off*.'

The one with the cigarette snorted again.

The pug didn't look pleased. 'What you doing mixing with Abby pond-life, Geeky? Trying to get your IQ down a bit?'

'Got another book on the go, Geeky?' The ginger reached out a hand for the Geek's book. 'Let's have a look at it.'

But as he went to grab it Sophie grabbed his wrist and held it tight.

The ginger looked at her hand holding his wrist and then at Sophie. 'Want to let go?'

'Want to leave his book alone?' Sophie dropped the boy's wrist.

'Getting rubbish from the council estate to stick up for you now, Geeky?' said the pug-nose.

'You're pretty tough guys, aren't you?' Sophie said. 'Three onto one.'

The lad with the cigarette snorted again, louder.

The ginger stared hard into Sophie's eyes. She didn't blink. 'Forget it,' he said. 'Let's leave them to make some mutant offspring.' He turned away and kicked a pebble in front of him. The pug-nose turned too and they headed back towards the school. Only the smoker stayed for a moment to look at Sophie. He dropped his cigarette on the dirt path and stamped it out. Then he popped his lips at her before turning and joining his mates.

'Weird,' Sophie said.

'Thanks,' said the Geek.

'Don't mention it,' said Sophie. 'Actually I was bit scared he was going to –'

'I mean thanks, thanks a bunch, because now you've just *made things much worse* for me.'

With that he stuffed his book in his rucksack and scuttled off towards the footbridge crossing the brook.

2

The dreams had started when she was almost twelve and they came to Sophie on an irregular basis. She might have the dreams every night for a week and then none for a few months. Sometimes she could hardly remember them. Sometimes they didn't seem like dreams at all, just scraps of information. She learned to distinguish between what she called *shimmering* dreams and real, ordinary dreams. If you can call a dream about flying on an elephant's back at the seaside while an orchestra made their noses stretch like trombones an ordinary real dream, that is.

But the shimmers were different. It was like they were a message, but in a language she didn't understand. When she'd dreamed of a wall with the words 'The Time Has Come' that's all it was. Ordinary dreams usually had a beginning and a middle and no end. The shimmers had no beginning, no middle and no end.

That evening Sophie was stuck on her maths homework so she got her dad to help her, even though he wasn't much assistance.

'Wait a minute,' her dad said. 'If x = y, then . . . what did you say x was?' Sophie's dad worked for the water authority. He had a weird job. Sometimes he had to go out and listen for underground leaks. He had very good hearing. Sometimes he had to get up early when there was no traffic around and listen hard for water rushing under the road. Then the workmen would come and fix the broken pipe. He was very good at his job. He was just pretty useless at maths.

'That's not the question, Dad.'

'So if x equals y and z is the . . . what was the formula?' Her dad had close-cropped hair and large flappy ears; though he said the large flappy nature of his ears had nothing to do with his remarkable listening skills.

'Look, Dad, you're missing the point!'

'What you getting cross with me for? I'm trying to help you!'

'You're barking up the wrong tree, Dad!'

'Oh, so I'm a dog now, am I?'

'No! I'm just saying! Look, Dad!'

And that's pretty much how it went for an hour, with Sophie's dad trying to help but just making difficult maths homework pretty impossible. Like most dads. Sophie thought that he'd be more help if he didn't try to help.

Anyway, when they'd finally decided on the value of x and the formula for y, Sophie packed her schoolbag for the next day, wondering how she was going to tackle the Geek. All she needed to know was what the book was about and who had written it, so that she could get a copy for herself in the hope that it might reveal something about her shimmering dream.

But now the Geek was less likely to want to talk to her than ever.

Of course Sophie was pleased about the way she'd stood up to the Geek's tormentors. The truth was that her heart had been beating so fast during the confrontation that she thought she was going to throw up. Luckily for her she'd been taught how to disguise her emotions. Those bullies were like cowardly pack animals: they looked for fear. When they hadn't found it in Sophie they hadn't known what to do.

But it hadn't helped her get any closer to the Geek. In fact he was more likely to avoid her now than before. Before going to bed that night she logged onto the internet and ran a search for the book title. A couple of books did come up with the same title, but they were completely different: one was about financial dealings in China and one about the Bible. They certainly weren't the paperback novel that the Geek was reading. Somehow she was going to have to get her hands on that book.

The next morning she left for school a little earlier than usual, planning to station herself at the corner of the street that joined Parkland Drive. When she saw the Geek coming, once again with his nose in a book, she planned her walk so that they would arrive at the corner of the street at the same moment. No way could he ignore her.

'Oh God, not you!' said the Geek. He flipped his book shut and quickened his step.

'Good morning to you, too, matie,' she said, keeping pace with him

'Please leave me alone.'

'Huh? Do you own the street then? I have to walk to school this way, too, you know.'

'Well, walk behind me a bit.'

'What do you think I am? Your Indian bride, seven paces behind you?'

'Well, walk in front then!'

'I'd have to run and skip, the pace you're going!'

'Well, walk to the side, cross the street, go in

front, go behind, I just don't care. But don't walk with me.'

'Why not?'

'Because you have no idea how much stick I will get today 'cos of that incident last night. No idea.'

'Stick? What are you afraid of? So they'll call you a few names. You can't crawl into a hole just because they call you a few names.'

The Geek stopped and turned to Sophie. 'Are you still here?' Then he turned to the sky. 'She is. She's still here. Why? I don't know. But she's still here!'

Sophie laughed. 'What are you afraid of?'

'I'm certainly not afraid.'

'Yes, you are. You're afraid of being seen walking with a girl. Particularly a girl from Abby, who you think is beneath you. You're afraid of your own shadow.'

'I am certainly *not afraid of my own shadow*!' the Geek shouted.

Sophie was surprised by this sudden burst of anger. 'Ease up!' she said. 'I'm only teasing.'

The Geek started walking again. Sophie kept pace with him. He took his glasses off and ran a hand through his mop of curls, and Sophie thought: *You know what? He's quite cute behind those glasses.*

'Can I ask you a question?' Sophie said. They were walking incredibly fast.

'Oh God!'

'Just one question.'

He sighed, and she took that for a yes.

'That book you have there. Is it the same one you were reading yesterday?'

'Yes,' he said, eyeing her suspiciously. 'Why?'

'I'm interested in books.'

'Really.'

'Oh yes. Love reading. Love it. Always on the lookout for new books.'

'Really.'

'Oh yes. Can't get enough books. Love them. All of them. Fat ones, thin ones, long ones, short ones, in fact –'

'Are you taking the micky?'

'No! Honestly!' Sophie realised she might have been laying it on a bit thick. 'What I mean is . . . I'm always on the lookout for a new book. Do we really have to walk this fast?'

Sophie's real concern was that by the time they reached the washbrook footbridge she would be joined by Suki on her way to school. She had to get the information she needed from the Geek before Suki scared him off. She was relieved when his pace slowed slightly.

'What kind of a book is it?' she asked.

'It's a ghost story. I've almost finished it. Here, look at it for yourself.'

Sophie's hand actually trembled slightly as she took the book from him. She flipped it over and looked at the cover. 'No,' she said, 'this isn't the book you were reading yesterday morning. I meant the one you had when you bumped into me.'

'Yes, that's the one.'

'No, it isn't.'

'Yes, it is.'

'No, it isn't.'

'You're mad! Completelyvmad! I've been reading this book for a week! You'd think I'd know which one it was! But no! You seem to know better than me what I've been reading.'

The book in Sophie's hand was called *The Tide Has Gone*. In frustration she turned the book over and scanned the back of it. Then she flipped through the pages. She must have misread it. Maybe that was possible. After all, she'd been so shocked by the weirdness of the words from her dream manifesting themselves on the wall that she was probably slightly dazed. She could easily have mistaken the title of the book in the moment that she had glanced at it. 'You're absolutely sure?'

'Of course I'm sure. Is that girl waving at you?

19

You'd better go on ahead and join her.'

Sophie glanced up. It was Suki and she was indeed waving.

'You're right,' said Sophie. 'And I must be going mad. I thought it was called *The Time Has Come*. And what made me so interested in it was . . .'

The Geek looked sideways at her. 'Was what?'

For no reason that she would ever understand, Sophie took a deep breath and decided to tell him. 'The brick wall by the school. I thought someone had painted the same words in white paint. Then at the end of the day it was gone. Like you say, I'm going mad.'

The Geek stopped, turned, took off his glasses and looked hard at her. 'No, you're not,' he said. 'I saw it on the wall, too.'

Sophie was shocked. She had so little time to discuss it with the Geek because Suki was waiting for them not more than ten yards away. She just had time to ask the Geek if he'd dreamed the same thing the night before. He nodded briefly.

'We'll be late,' Suki shouted, 'if you guys don't get a move on.' When the Geek wasn't looking she wrinkled her nose and squinted at Sophie as if to ask her what she was doing.

'This is my friend Suki,' Sophie said.

The Geek groaned. 'Oh God,' he said. 'There's another one.'

'Who's this?' Suki said. 'What's he on about?'

Sophie was about to introduce him as the Geek, but stopped herself in time. 'Well, what is your name anyway?'

'What have I done to deserve this?' he said to no one in particular. 'It's James.'

'Well, James always walks this way so I said he could walk with us,' Sophie said by way of explanation.

'Oh please no!' James moaned softly. 'Anything but that.'

'No,' Suki said breezily. 'You wouldn't want to be seen walking with *pond-life*, would you?'

Pond-life. It was what some of the superior boys from Leicester Castle called the girls at Abby.

'It's not that at all,' James protested angrily. 'I've never called you that.'

'Then stop moaning,' Suki said. 'Most boys would be glad to walk to school with two pretty girls.'

'And here comes Amy,' said Sophie.

'For pity's sake,' James said. 'There's three of them.'

Amy arrived, barely seeming to notice James. She was too busy asking the others if they'd found last

21

night's maths homework difficult. Amy said she'd asked her dad to help but he was pretty useless. Suki said hers was too. Sophie suddenly had an idea that the Geek – that is, James – might be a whiz at maths, so she asked him.

'I have to go,' said James. 'Really, I do.'

'Look,' said Sophie, 'we have to talk.'

James looked pained. 'Right,' he said. 'Right.' Then he was crossing the road, trying to distance himself from the girls before anyone else saw him.

'What's going on?' Amy wanted to know.

Sophie was a pretty honest kind of person but on this occasion it was just too difficult to tell her friends about the dream, the book, the wall and about the fact that James had seen the writing on the wall, too. So she swallowed and told a barefaced lie. 'My mum knows his mum. He doesn't have any friends so she asked if I'd walk with him to school occasionally.'

'Poor you,' said Amy.

'Yeh,' said Suki. 'Poor you.'

3

There was a wooden bench in the graveyard at the church of Mary Magdalene. It was hidden from all the kids – from either school – who might pass by the church on their way towards the washbrook. A giant yew tree spread its ancient and dusky arms behind the bench and a privet hedge shielded it from view on one side. You had to take the narrow path behind the church to even see that the bench was there.

After school, Sophie had persuaded James to meet her there. She'd intercepted him on his way home again, but had suggested that he make his own way there to avoid the embarrassing consequences of being seen walking with a specimen of Abby pond-life. Plus she hadn't been able to think of any other suitable place to meet. She certainly wasn't going to suggest the derelict farmhouse waiting for demolition: it had a reputation as a snogging venue, at least for those who weren't completely creeped out by the place. The church graveyard seemed quite a cheerful alternative by comparison.

She'd let him go ahead and had expected him to already be there when she arrived. But he wasn't. She sat down on the bench and waited.

Sophie sat reading inscriptions on the mossy headstones. Some of them were so old they were completely worn away. Others had peculiar names: *Lydia Liquorice, died 1872. Gone Before.*

Before what? thought Sophie.

It was peaceful in the graveyard. It was late spring and the afternoon sunlight warmed the grey stone of the church. The shouts and chatter of schoolkids on their way home had died away. A robin swooped onto a nearby headstone and seemed to look at her. She began to think that James had changed his mind and wasn't coming. She decided to give him another ten minutes.

She was about to leave when she heard something stirring behind one of the gravestones. It was a sudden flutter. The she heard a breathing sound. After a moment James's head popped from behind the headstone.

'What are you doing?' Sophie cried.

'Shhhh! We don't want people to hear us.'

'Look, I don't mind being careful, but I'm not going to go creeping about just because you're ashamed of being seen with a girl. You could just come down the path like an ordinary human being. Why are you so late?'

He sat down on the bench beside her, took his glasses off and wiped his face with his hand. He had a leaf stuck in his hair from clambering through the bushes. 'Oh, the usual.'

Sophie guessed that his tormenters had been at him again, throwing his books around.

'You can stand up to them, you know.'

He blinked at her.

'I learned how. You can learn how, too.'

'I don't want to talk about it,' said James. 'And anyway, you didn't get me to come here to talk about that.'

'No,' Sophie said. 'You're right. The wall. You said you'd seen what was painted there. Tell me what you saw.'

'Well, it was weird. I'd dreamed it before I saw it. It was white paint on the brick wall.'

'White, yes, with letters about three feet high?'

'Yes! And it just said, "The Time Has Come". And then later it was gone.'

'That's exactly what I saw,' Sophie said. 'What's more, I've asked all my friends if they saw it. But no one did. Yet you couldn't miss it. It was screaming at you. So how come only you and I saw it?'

'There is an answer,' said James, 'but I don't want to tell you what it is.'

'If you don't,' Sophie said, 'I might just slap you.'

James looked around him, as if there might be one of his enemies lurking in the graveyard, hiding behind one of the tombstones. The sun was going down behind the church spire, throwing them into shadow. 'First, I want you to tell me what other things have happened like this.'

Sophie told him all about the dreams that were not dreams: what she called the *shimmers*. She thought it might take some time to explain, but James seemed to know exactly what she was talking about. He asked her when these things started happening, and she told him.

'Same with me,' he said. 'About the time I started getting acne.'

Sophie laughed. 'You can be funny!' she said.

But James wasn't smiling. 'What's funny about acne?'

'Sorry. Go on. You said you could tell me what's going on.'

'All I can tell you is what I've read. I read a lot of books and –'

'Yeh, I noticed you like books.'

'If you keep interrupting me I'm just going to go.'

'Hey! A bit touchy, aren't you?'

James looked away, as if hurt. Sophie suddenly realised something about him. 'James, don't you have many friends?' she said.

He shook his head sadly.

'Well, maybe you've got one now,' she said. 'But *not* if you're going to snap at me.'

He sighed. 'Okay, I read a lot of books. I've read everything I can. I've raided every second-hand bookshop, every charity bookshop, every library sale, every discount bookstore. It started with anything to do with dreams, but it expanded to cover anything to do with ghosts, spirits, vampires, unicorns, fairies, demons, anything I could get hold of. It's a collection. My dad calls it the Black Library.'

'Where do you live?'

'Behind the race-course. I live with my dad. My mum left us when I was three. We do okay.'

'Did I say you didn't?'

'Huh? No. But anyway, all these things, fairies, demons, ghosts – they all come from the same place. One book I read called it the Corridor. Another called it the Waiting Room. Anyway, it's where you go when you have those special dreams, what you called the shimmers. It's the same place, believe me.'

A kind of sigh crept around the graveyard and a

shiver passed through Sophie. 'How can you be sure?'

'I told you. I go there, too.'

The sun had disappeared behind the church now, and the temperature had dropped. The bench they sat on was in shadow and the giant spreading yew tree behind them suddenly seemed gloomy and hostile rather than protective. Sophie felt chilled. She stood up and hugged herself. 'Let's walk on.'

James looked like he would have preferred to stay where he was.

Sophie knew what was bothering him. 'It's all right. All the other kids have long gone. Nobody will see us together.'

He got up from the bench and they walked back down the gravel path and out of the churchyard. 'I'm not ashamed of being seen with you,' he said.

'Wow! I'm honoured.'

James got cross. 'You always deliberately take me the wrong way! You do it on purpose!'

'Calm down, will you! You have to get used to a bit of teasing!'

'What I meant was I'm not at all ashamed of being seen with you, but if I do get seen with you they'll make my life hell.'

'What will they do?'

'Oh, push me around, call me names. Tease me

about having a girlfriend.'

'You should be so lucky, eh? Anyway, what are we going to do about it all?'

'What? About them thinking you're my girl-friend?'

'No, you *drong*! About these dreams. About these messages.'

'I don't know if there is anything you can do about them. I just get the feeling that something is going to happen.'

'You mean in all of your books there's nothing to tell you what you can do?'

'Well, there *are* things you can do. You can go looking for things. Tell me something, have you ever had any strange visits?'

When James said those words Sophie felt a chime, like from a very old and very distant bell located somewhere deep inside her. And yet she had no idea what James was talking about.

'What do you mean by visitors?'

'Oh. You'd know it if you had. I have a feeling you'll get a visit pretty soon.'

'A visit from who?'

'Whom. You should say: a visit from *whom*.'

'Are you mad? Is this an English lesson? Who is going to visit me?'

'Well, it's like this. One evening I was doing my

homework on the kitchen table. I had all my books spread on the table. I was feeling a bit tired so I put my head on the table and the next second the doorbell went.'

'You're scaring me, a bit,' said Sophie.

'I don't mean to.'

Suddenly there was a cry from a distance. 'GEEEEEEEEK!!!!!!' A couple of stragglers from Castle in their claret blazers had spotted him.

'I'm off,' he said. 'I'll talk to you some more tomorrow morning on the way to school.'

'No, you won't,' said Sophie.

'Why not?'

'Tomorrow is Saturday. No school.'

James ran a hand through his mass of curls. 'Monday then. Monday.'

'Wait!' Sophie said. 'Don't just run off!'

But he was gone.

4

Sophie looked forward to Friday evenings, because every week she went to judo training sessions at the local leisure centre. She was already a blue belt and could throw most boys her own age. Though Sophie wasn't stupid enough to believe that judo was the same as real fighting, the art had given her a confidence that not everyone had.

Her teacher – or sensei, to give him the proper Japanese term –was a calm, grey-haired man with a slight squint in one eye. William Trafford was a former British champion. 'Remember, Sophie, that judo means the Subtle Way. Don't ever think that knowing a few throws can stop you being beaten up. This isn't the movies. But what it can always do is buy you enough time to –'

'To run,' said Sophie.

William smiled. 'That's right. If you can surprise someone by stopping them dead in their tracks or throwing them, then you just get the hell out of there. Now step onto the mat while we're waiting for the others to arrive.'

The room in which judo was practised was called a dojo and you always had to bow to the sensei, which had made Sophie feel a bit silly at first but she quickly got used to it. The regime in the dojo was quite strict. You had to bow to all the black belts when they came in. There was no talking or giggling allowed while on the mat. But William never had to ask anyone for silence. He had his 'bulldog': a younger man with a short black beard who would keep everyone in order. Meanwhile William only had to let his gaze fall on someone and they would go quiet.

Another thing William had told her was that sometimes not looking afraid, standing tall and relaxed, could be enough to put off a bully or an aggressor. 'These are signals, tiny signals, sometimes you don't even see them, but they have an effect,' William explained. Sometimes she thought William was being mysterious when he said these things. If you couldn't see a signal, then how could it be a signal? But William had told her to trust her intuition.

'Sometimes you might think an opponent is going to throw you to the right, but your intuition is telling you he's going the other way. He's tricking you. You need to train your intuition, because your body often knows things before your mind does.'

'How can you train your intuition?' Sophie asked.

'Practice,' said William. He stepped left as if to reach for Sophie and she responded quickly, trying to wrong-foot her master. But William had already gone to the other side, and with Sophie off balance William threw her easily by a simple prod to the shoulder.

'I wasn't ready!' Sophie protested.

'Your mind was listening, but your body wasn't,' William laughed. 'Come on, try again.'

Sophie wanted to tell William about how she'd stood up to James's bullies after school; but she wasn't sure how William would react. He might be cross with her. He taught avoidance. Confrontation was not always the way with judo, and that's exactly what Sophie had done: she'd met James's tormentors head on, and at some risk to herself. This time it had worked. Another time – well, who could say about another time?

The session went swiftly. Sophie practised her ground work, which basically involved grappling with someone on the floor and using your arms and legs to hold them down. She had the bad luck to be paired with a boy called Simon who hadn't discovered how to use deodorant on his underarms. For a few moments she had her nose locked in his armpit and she thought she was going to faint. Sophie was too good-natured to mention it but was relieved when she swapped partners. Simon's next partner was a boy called Johnno who wasn't as tactful as Sophie.

'Simon, you are rank! Your pits stink like a ferret's cage!' Johnno shouted. 'I ain't doin' ground work with you!'

'Okay,' William said diplomatically, 'I think Simon might have got the message.'

At the end of the session Sophie had a word with William. 'I might bring a friend along with me next week.'

'Of course. All welcome. What's her name?'

'It's a he.'

'A-ha!' William said. 'A boy. I see.'

'No, it's nothing like that!' Sophie protested.

William pretended to be shocked. 'Did I even say it was?'

'No, but I was using my . . . intuition.'

William smiled his secretive smile. 'You know what, Sophie. You're too darned smart. Of course he can come. What's his name?'

'James. Although I don't know if he wants to come. I just think it would be a good idea.'

'Well, you can't exactly put him in a headlock and

make him come if he doesn't want to. It doesn't work like that.'

Sophie told William what she knew about James being bullied. William listened. 'Okay, bring him along if he's willing. We'll take a look at him.'

Sophie was already determined that she would get James along to judo. She didn't think it would be easy, but she thought it would be good for his self confidence. She went home from the dojo scheming about how she might persuade him.

On the way she had to stop and ask herself why it was important to her. She couldn't answer. It had something to do with the wall, and the writing on the wall.

The following afternoon she visited Suki, and stayed until about seven o'clock. They spent the time in Suki's bedroom. Suki had a pile of new cosmetics bought for her birthday, so they spent a couple of hours painting their faces. Then they washed it all off. Then they put it all on again.

Suki had her face practically pressed up against the mirror as she applied mascara. 'So what's with this boy, then?' she asked.

Sophie had to smile to herself. How clever of Suki to ask when she seemed to be so focused on some other task. But Sophie wasn't fooled. She knew Suki had been waiting to find a moment to press her.

'He's not like a boyfriend or anything.'

'Really? You spend a lot of time with him.'

Sophie was simply unable to say why. Instead she said, 'Well, there's two things. One, I feel a bit sorry for him, and two, he's really all right. When you get to know him.'

'Well, it seems like you prefer his company to mine and Amy's.'

'That's because –' Sophie was about to say that it was because James happened to walk past her front door to and from school every day, but she stopped. She stopped because she had seen something in the mirror.

It was a grey hand, resting lightly on Suki's shoulder. Her first thought, ridiculously, had been that it was a small and furry animal, like a gerbil or a rat, its fur bristling as it balanced itself against the collar of her friend's blouse. But it had moved to stroke the back of a long grey finger across the nape of Suki's neck.

Sophie was momentarily shocked into silence. Then the hand – if it had been a hand – was gone.

'What?' Suki said. Her own hand, containing the eyelash comb, fell to her side. She turned and looked at Sophie. 'What is it?'

Sophie was suddenly struck by the impression that her friend seemed tired, drained even. Her normally healthy glow was absent. Her usually golden skin seemed a little grey. 'Nothing. It's silly. He's not my boyfriend. We don't snog or anything.'

Suki went back to applying black mascara to her eyelashes. 'I do with mine,' she said.

'Oh! Didn't even know you had one! Who is it?'

'Mind your biz,' Suki said a little sharply. 'You don't tell me anything, so I don't tell you anything.'

Suki was shutting her out. That remark, and the apparition of a hand at Suki's shoulder, had soured the evening for Sophie. She went back for supper, watched some TV with her folks and went to bed.

And under the cosy duvet Sophie could almost have dismissed that thing – that chilling grey hand playing at her friend's shoulders – as a trick of the mirror's light. It could have been a perfectly ordinary Saturday evening.

Ordinary until around midnight, that is.

With the house in darkness and her parents asleep, Sophie popped awake. She looked at the red LED on her digital clock. It was one minute before midnight. A strange silver light was streaming through the window. She moved the curtain aside and there was a brilliant moon, but someone or something had taken a large bite out of it. There were teethmarks in the moon, just as if it had been a soft cheese.

Sophie got out of bed and glanced into her parents' room. They slept soundly. She crept downstairs and found their lurcher dog, Tasha, standing by the front door. This was odd because normally Tasha stayed in her basket in the kitchen.

The doorbell sounded.

I'm dreaming this, thought Sophie.

Because she knew this was a dream, she opened the door. A tall man stood at the door, holding a wooden tray in front of him. He had wild hair and a straggly beard and a high wind blew his hair across his face. Yet the wind wasn't blowing anywhere else. The bushes and the cherry tree outside Sophie's house were not registering even a breath of wind. Somehow this was the man's *personal storm*.

Sophie felt a thrill of fear chase through her.

She almost wanted to laugh, but out of nervous terror. The wind-blown man wore a long grey coat, and the moonlight gleamed on his silver buttons. He had a number of objects on the tray in front of him, but Sophie couldn't tell what any of them were. The man was holding something out towards her. His hands were huge, wrinkled like leather and with strong blue veins. There was dirt under his fingernails. In his hands was a note and he wanted Sophie to take it.

She took the note. It was blank. She turned it over, and the other side was blank. She turned it back again. This time there was something written on the note. It read: *this is not a dream.*

'Who are you?' Sophie thought. That is, she believed she'd only thought it and not spoken it aloud, but the man answered her.

'The hawker,' he said. Except that his lips didn't move when he spoke; or if they did move they did so way too late, long after he'd said those two words.

He held the tray towards her. He wanted her to take something, but everything was wrapped in brown paper and it was impossible to even guess what each object might be. Eventually she took something disc-shaped.

Then the hawker held out his hand again, but palm up, like someone who wanted paying. She felt in her pyjama pocket and took out a silver button she'd never seen before. It was a large button with fancy engraving, though it had a portion missing, exactly like the moon when she'd looked out of the window. She handed the button over. The hawker accepted it and placed it in his pocket.

Tasha panted and looked up at her, but her dog's eyes were now like silver moons, or silver buttons. When she looked back, the hawker had gone. Sophie closed the door and went back to bed.

When she woke in the morning, the dream – if that is what it was – seemed so real to her she looked for the paper-wrapped package that the hawker had given her. But she couldn't find it anywhere. She went downstairs and had breakfast in her pyjamas. Her dad was up and about already. She thought about telling him her dream, but she decided against it.

Sophie's dad made her a bacon sandwich. He drove her mad with his singing. For a man with such good hearing he didn't exactly have a good voice, but she never said anything because it meant he was in a good mood. He banged the pan onto the stove and set the bacon sizzling.

'Tea, your highness?' he asked her.

That was another thing that drove her mad.

'Tea, imported from the distant subcontinent of India to her very highness's door, steeped in hot water by her royal servants, served with milk fresh from the cow in the pasture of her highness's meadows –'

'Shaddup, Dad! I'm not in the mood!'

'– all for her highness's pleasure and refreshment and . . . here, what's this?'

With the bacon sizzling on the hob he held up a scrap of paper he'd found on the kitchen worktop. 'Is this yours?'

He handed it to her. It was a dirty old square scrap of paper. On one side of it was written the words: *this is not a dream.*

5

Sunday dragged. It dragged like a ship's anchor lodged in a mud bank at low tide. Sophie had never known a day go so slow, and she'd never been so keen for Monday to come around. She didn't hate school, but even so, the last night of the weekend always left a heavy feeling in the pit of her stomach. Plus her little spat with Suki bothered her more than it should have done. It was only a small thing but Sophie felt that it was the kind of thing that could grow. Something was wrong.

But there was a reason why she wanted to hurry things along. Because she had to go and talk to James. Because she knew now what he'd meant by having a visitor.

It bothered her that she didn't even know where James lived. All he'd said was 'behind the race-course'. Well, that narrowed it down to any one of about six hundred houses in several dozen streets.

She had no street name, no house number, no landmark, nothing. Of course, she had no telephone number for him either. She didn't even know his surname, or she might have looked it up in the telephone directory for a clue.

If she'd known where James lived she would have gone to his home, knocked on his door and asked to talk with him. That was how disturbed she'd been by that crazy image of the wind-blown hawker. It would have been okay if she could have dismissed it as a dream. But there was the scrap of paper, the note.

Sophie had turned that scrap of paper over and over, trying to extract every detail from it. To be sure, it looked like a perfectly ordinary piece of plain white paper, though it had a cream-coloured tinge. It was quite thick, and she'd even torn it slightly to see what it was made of. Tearing it was not easy because the paper seemed slightly waxy, but it was after all possible to tear it if she'd wanted to. It was creased in places, and whether that was from her handling of it, or from her father's handling of it, or whether it had been like that when the hawker handed it over, she didn't know. As for the words, they seemed to be written in ordinary black ink, though when she tried to gently smear the ink with a wet finger the writing resisted and refused to

43

smudge altogether. The words were written in neat handwriting, with even letters. The only thing she thought unusual about it was that there was no capital letter T to start the sentence, and no full stop: *this is not a dream*

Sophie knew that the visit from the hawker was another shimmer. It was the most vivid and most strange shimmer that she'd ever experienced. It made her feel strange and light-headed, and yet at the same time with a weight in her stomach.

If only she could talk to James about it, he might help her to explain what it all meant, what was happening to her. She couldn't tell her mum or dad. They would become worried and anxious about her. They might even whisk her off to see a doctor. She heard her dad singing loudly as he took a cup of tea up to where her mum was still in bed, and decided that they just weren't able to help her.

But events were about to become stranger. Just as Sophie's mum was about to serve up a traditional Sunday lunch of roast lamb and Yorkshire pudding, the doorbell sounded.

'Get that, will you, Sophie?' her mum called to her. 'I don't want this gravy to stick.'

Sophie went to the door and when she opened it she felt the blood drain from her face just as surely as if it had been sucked out of her by a vampire. It was a hawker. With a basket of goods.

"Ello, sweetheart, how are you? Is your mum in?'

'Busy,' was all that Sophie could croak. True, the hawker wasn't the same as the man in the dream, but he looked like a near version of him. He was smaller, and his beard was shorter and more of a ginger colour than the night hawker's. Instead of a tray he had a wicker basket. He had no wind blowing across his face either and he talked normally. He wasn't the same exactly, but he was too powerfully similar altogether for Sophie not to be almost struck dumb.

The man at the door smiled, rearranging the things in his basket as he spoke. 'How about your dad then, my darlin', has he got a moment, eh? Tell him I'd like a word.'

Sophie ducked back inside and called her dad. He came through from the living room. 'Who is it?'

Sophie just pointed.

Sophie's dad went to the door to be met by a barrage of talk. 'Mornin', sir, or afternoon I should say, isn't that right? I'm just keeping myself busy, you know, out of trouble, that's it, selling me wares, keeping out of trouble and –'

'No thanks,' said her dad. He didn't have much time for door-to-door salesmen of any kind.

'You've helped me out in the past,' said the hawker, 'and I wondered if you could again, cos I've got –'

'No.'

'– dusters, cloths, wipers, clothes lines, pegs, tea towels –

'No.'

'– tea cosies, look at that, knitted by disabled kiddies, isn't that nice, makes you laugh, coasters, I've got coasters, chamois leathers, look at these shoe brushes, small enough to take with you when you go away –'

'No thanks.'

'– have a look through the basket, go on, bound to be something you need, shoelaces, need bootlaces? Keeps me out of trouble, keeps me out of mischief –'

'No.'

'Buy something, Dad!' Sophie, hovering behind her dad in the doorway, almost shouted this.

'What a nice gal!' shouted the hawker, breaking into a huge smile and showing plenty of gaps where his teeth should be. 'I said to myself she was a lovely gal when she came to the door. You've got to buy something now. You've gotta!'

'No, I haven't!'

The hawker laughed and stamped his foot and winked at Sophie. 'He has, hasn't he, darlin'? He has!'

'Buy something,' Sophie said, softly this time but insistently.

'Dinner's on the table,' Mum called to them.

Dad gave in. 'Pick something out,' he told Sophie.

She stepped forward, a little nervously, to look into the basket. The hawker started sorting through his basket, turning things over. He seemed to be pushing something towards her.

'What's that?' she said.

'Chamois leather. Good choice.'

She picked it up. 'What's it for?'

'Cleaning windows, cleaning your car, don't need no detergent, do it, sir, very good choice. Smart girl.'

'Go on then,' Dad said. 'We'll have it.'

Sophie didn't feel she'd had chance to have a good look through the basket, but her dad was already asking how much.

'Just five pounds, that one, sir.'

'Five? Bloody hell!'

'Top quality. Top quality. Rot-proof. Good size. Just the five, that one.'

Dad found a fiver in his pocket but was scratching his head as he handed it over. The hawker was already hoisting the handle of his big wicker basket into the crook of his arm and getting ready to move on.

'Dinner's on the table!' Mum called again.

When her dad turned to go back indoors the hawker stepped forward and whispered to Sophie, very rapidly, 'Don't let go of it.'

Sophie wondered what he meant, but she didn't get a chance to ask him. He was already on his way, cheerfully intent on charming a fiver out of the Robinsons who lived in the house next door.

'Who was that?' Mum asked as they sat down to dinner.

'A door-to-door pedlar,' Dad said, tucking into his roast lamb. 'I almost had him on his way before *your daughter* called him back and made me give him five pounds.' Sophie was always *your daughter* when one or other of her parents had cause to complain.

'Oh well. What did you buy?'

Sophie showed her the chamois leather.

'He gave the old sob story about staying out of trouble,' Dad said.

'Oh, that old story,' said Mum. 'I expect Sophie felt sorry for him.'

'What sob story?'

'Well, when they say they're staying out of trouble they're saying that if they weren't busy selling all this tat they'd be robbing your house or your car. You're supposed to congratulate them for not doing anything illegal.'

'I expect he's just trying to get by,' said Mum.

'Fair enough,' said Dad, 'but you don't have to feel sorry for everyone who comes to the door.'

Sophie hadn't felt sorry for the hawker at all. She'd just felt deep down that she had to buy something from him. She couldn't believe that the arrival of the hawker was unconnected with the shimmer that had happened in the night.

Dad put his knife and fork down and picked up the chamois leather. 'You have to laugh,' he said. 'Five quid for this. They're about two pounds in the shops, if that.' He flapped the square of leather open. 'And would you believe it! It's got holes in it!'

Eyebrows raised, he turned his gaze onto Sophie. She reddened.

'Mint sauce, anyone?' said Mum.

6

'No,' said James. He took off his glasses and looked hard at her. 'That isn't the same visitor that I had. Mine was a . . .' He tailed off.

'What?' Sophie had made sure that she'd set off for school early that morning in order to intercept James. Even though it threatened rain and gusts of wind chased swirling eddies of dust and leaves up the street.

'Never mind. It was still a visitor all the same. Come on, we don't want to be late.'

Sophie knew what he meant: let's be so early no one will see us together. 'But what does it mean?' she wailed at him.

'I can only tell you what I've read and heard about,' said James. 'But you won't like it.'

'Try me.'

'You're a *savant*. Like I am.'

'A what? What the heck is one of those?'

'You'll have to meet Mrs Royston. She'll explain it to you. I can't really.'

'Who is Mrs Royston?'

'A neighbour. She's like three hundred years old. Well, okay, not quite. But she knows all about these things.'

'Things? What things? You're not making any sense. I've waited all weekend to ask you some questions and now you're just talking rubbish!'

'Excuse me! Am I the one who chases you home from school? Am I the one who waits behind the bushes to jump out at you in the morning? Am I the one who insists on mysterious appointments in weird places like . . . like . . . graveyards? Am I the one stalking your every move?'

'Stalking??'

'Yes, stalking. You're like a damned stalker!' And with that James hurried down the street.

Sophie was so taken aback by his outburst that she let him go on. She followed him to school but about twenty yards behind him. When she approached the footbridge over the washbrook she saw, through a gap between the houses, that Suki was already there waiting. She could see that there was a boy or a young man with her. He wore a long coat. They were leaning on the rail of the foot-bridge looking down into the water. The young man, it seemed to Sophie, had his arm around Suki. As Sophie hurried on, her view of her friend was interrupted by trees and houses.

And when she rounded the corner of the avenue, the young man was no longer there.

Suki looked up as Sophie approached the bridge. 'Hey,' Suki said. 'Your geeky friend just came by, talking to himself fifteen to the dozen.'

'Really?' Sophie said, looking round for the boy, though there was now no trace of him.

'He's a bit odd, if you ask me,' Suki said.

'Yeh,' Sophie said. 'A bit odd.'

At the end of the school day Sophie didn't even bother looking for James. She felt a little stung by his 'stalker' remarks. She was a pretty girl, and she didn't want anyone to think that she spent her time chasing boys who didn't want to be caught; or chasing any kind of boys for that matter. The truth was that she'd felt a bit sorry for James and almost felt like she was doing him a favour.

Now she'd learned that sometimes people don't want your favours.

But it was more complicated than that. James happened to be the one person who, like her, had seen the writing appear on the wall before it disappeared again. Then it had seemed like he was the one person who could possibly give her some answers about the strange things that were happening in her life.

Yet he didn't want anything to do with her.

She walked home with Amy and Suki that evening determined not even to look at any claret blazer walking near by. Even when she thought she spotted James across the road from the church she managed not to miss a beat in her conversation with the girls.

'Looking for your bit of hot stuff?' Amy teased.

'Yeh, geek boy. Where is he?' said Suki.

Sophie shrugged. 'No idea.'

'Well,' said Suki, and there was an unusually mean note in her voice, 'Sophie won't want to come where we're going.'

'Suppose not,' Amy giggled.

'She'll be too busy getting it on with geek boy. What do you do for fun – squeeze his acne spots?'

Sophie was open-mouthed. It was just so unlike Suki to be unkind. It was out of character and Sophie recovered enough to tell her so. 'You never used to be so mean, Suki! What's got into you?'

Suki simply waved away Sophie's words. 'Come on, Amy, we've got places to go.'

After her two friends had gone Sophie made her way home. Suki's words had made her feel cross about everything. She was still fighting an instinct to look for James but refrained from turning round or from looking up the street to see if he might be behind her or ahead of her; she avoided eye contact with a group of lads from Castle who may or may not have been the bullies from last week; and she even made herself look down at the ground when someone in a Castle blazer went by on a bicycle.

She was hell-bent and with gritted teeth determined not to care for one single second about James the Geek. She would, she decided, find out what she needed to know all on her own.

'I'll ask her.'

Sophie almost jumped back in alarm. It was James. He'd waited on the street corner, just as she had, lurking behind a privet hedge before jumping out on her. Sophie was lost for words.

'Mrs Royston. I'll ask her if I can take you to see her.'

'Okay,' Sophie said feebly.

'Bye,' said James.

'Bye.'

'Come on,' said Sophie's mum. 'Do your chores – then you can relax for the evening.'

'Amy doesn't have chores. Or Suki. Amy's dad just gives her ten pounds a week for doing nothing.'

'Yes, well, I'm not Amy's dad,' said Sophie's

mum, which was of course blindingly obvious, but which seemed to be one of her favourite sayings.

'I hate doing chores!'

'You don't have to do them. You just don't get any pocket money if you don't.'

'It's not fair.'

'But it is fair. It's very fair. It's exactly why we ask you to do some bits around the house: 'cos it's fair. And if you don't do them I'll get your dad to explain why we ask you to do them.'

Dad's *explanations* could go on for hours. They were worse than having to do the chores. He always started out by saying that life was divided between work, rest and play, by which time Sophie was already yawning. Then he went on to say that everyone should have a fair chance at each of work, rest and play, by which time Sophie was pretending to have fallen asleep. Then he spoke about how young people were lucky that they didn't have to do much work and that they got to go to school, to learn instead of work, and how he wished he could. By which time Sophie said things like 'You don't call listening for water work, do you?', to which he would reply, patiently, 'Sophie, you try getting up at five in the morning to listen for water.' And then he went on about how there was work around the house for Mum and even though Mum did the lion's share, she could do with some help from time to time and –

In fact Sophie had a sneaking suspicion about her dad. She thought that his habit of showing endless patience and mild-mannered long-winded explanations was a *trick*. His plan was to bore you into submission. You could stick your fingers in your ears and go *la-la-la-la-not-listening!* but when you took your fingers out again he'd still be talking away. You could go upstairs and he'd follow you up and push his way into the room, still lecturing you. You could lock yourself in the bathroom, and he'd sit outside, talking for England. Yes, it was a trick to bore you into submission, and it bloody well worked.

'He's in the lounge,' Sophie's mum said. 'Shall I ask him to come and explain it all again?'

'All right! What do you want doing? Anything but that!'

'You can hoover the living room and clean the windows, that would be a big help.'

Sophie knitted her brows and took the window-cleaning spray and cloths from under the sink. 'I'm just a servant round here. A drudge.'

'Yes, sweetheart,' said her mum. 'A princess turned into a serving wench. Here, use your new chamois leather.'

Sophie went through to the lounge. Dad had his

feet up on the sofa, reading the paper. He saw Sophie with the cleaning materials and opened his mouth to speak, but didn't get the chance.

'Don't say anything!' Sophie said.

Dad sat with his mouth open and nothing coming out, smiling pleasantly.

'And stop watching me!'

'Don't worry,' he said, getting up. 'I'm cooking the dinner tonight – you lucky things.'

That meant spaghetti bolognese, because he only ever had one dish on the menu, and off he went to prepare his magic-formula sauce. This left Sophie to get on with cleaning the windows on her own.

She shook out the wet chamois cloth that had come from the strange hawker. It comprised three scraps of chamois that had been stitched together, and Dad had been right – it did have a couple of small holes in it. But mum said they were famously good for cleaning windows and, better still, you didn't have to use detergent – just clean water.

The chamois squeaked pleasantly as Sophie rubbed it along the glass, and even though the window had seemed pretty clean a few smeary marks did seem to transfer themselves to the cloth. Anyway, it did make the glass shine. But then Sophie came across some tiny marks on the glass, and rubbing hard with the chamois cloth didn't seem to bring them off.

Sophie breathed on the glass and rubbed again. The marks seemed worse rather than better. Sophie wondered for a moment if the tiny white specks were actually scratch marks in the glass itself. She breathed on the glass again, leaving an oval-shaped pool of condensation from her breath. She rubbed vigorously with the cloth.

The marks were growing instead of shrinking. Every time she rubbed the specks with her cloth, they got bigger instead of smaller. They were actually coming off the cloth and onto the window.

'So much for this chamois leather!' Sophie said. She concluded that the modern methods were the best and decided to go back to using the detergent spray-gun and a dry cloth.

She was about to spray the flecked, dirty marks on the glass with a shot of Shine-O when the setting sun flared for a moment from between the neighbours' houses. Something stayed her hand. It was the marks themselves. In the sunlight it seemed to her that the little white flecks were not exactly random. That is, they seemed to have a pattern to them.

She squinted at the marks again. Once more she put her mouth close to the glass and breathed there. When she rubbed with the chamois leather again, there was no question about it: the marks were appearing more vivid, and larger. She breathed again, and rubbed with the leather cloth. The marks were forming into recognisable letters of the alphabet.

There was a mark followed by what might have been an A and then a speck and an N and maybe another A and some more specks and what could have been an E.

Sophie felt a shiver ripple through her skin. It was like a finger of ice had touched her neck.

She breathed on the marks in the glass again, misting them with condensation. She opened up the chamois leather and polished the glass hard, trying to clean the letters away. When she took the chamois off the glass, more letters had formed, clearer now. There was no doubt. An R, a V and an L. What's more a new, second word was forming underneath.

Sophie breathed on the glass, and rubbed. Breathed and rubbed. Breathed and rubbed.

She stood back. The first line of letters spelled out: *Ravendale*.

Underneath that was a new word: *Maslama*.

And even as she watched, a third word was forming there: *Picator*.

The sun setting behind the houses made the letters of the words seem to flare, almost to burn. But Sophie felt no warmth. She felt only a terrible weight in her stomach and a sudden, cold sense of loneliness. He tongue froze to the roof of her mouth. Even though it was not cold in the house, she could see her breath forming in front of her, like plumes of smoke on a misty February morning.

She dropped the leather to the floor and tried to shout out loud, but her voice was strangled in her throat. Only a small cry came out, but as it did the great plumes of steamy breath twisted and were sucked towards the flame-like words on the glass. And then the words themselves faded, not slowly but not in an instant either. Within seconds, the words had gone.

'Did you shout?' It was her mum.

Sophie turned. For a moment she was unable to speak.

'I thought you called me,' her mum said.

'I slipped,' said Sophie. 'I dropped the cloth.' She bent down to pick it up.

'Well,' said her mum. 'That looks much better. Leave it now and get on with the hoovering.'

'Is everything all right at school?' Mum wanted to know over dinner that evening.

'Yes.'

'You would say, wouldn't you? If something was bothering you?'

'Of course.'

'She looks a bit pale, doesn't she, Nick? Don't you think she looks a bit pale?'

'A bit,' said Sophie's dad. 'Perhaps it's my spag bol. Maybe she doesn't like it.' Dad was always fishing for compliments for this one dish he could cook. Always.

'It's fine,' said Sophie.

'Just fine? Not delicious, scrumptious and mouth-watering?'

'If you say so, Dad.'

'I do say so. I do. I say it myself.'

'I think you look a bit pale.'

'No, honestly, Mum, I'm fine. Really. Look at me, eating dad's spaghetti bolognese. Yum yum.'

Sophie had some history homework to do before bedtime, revising for a test the following day. But she couldn't concentrate on it. For one thing she was upset about what was happening with her best friends. Amy and Suki were off doing stuff they didn't even seem to want to tell her about. She felt squeezed out.

What's more, every time she looked at her textbook, all she could see were those three mysterious words, as if they'd been burned onto the pages before her. In truth they'd been burned into her memory. Even when she closed her eyes, the words burned brightly in her imagination, as if they had been embroidered in gold thread on a black velvet cloth: *Ravendale, Maslama, Picator*.

She tried running the words through a search engine, but in each case the words could be taken to mean several different things. There were lots of companies trading under the name of Ravendale. You could get Ravendale sewing machines or Ravendale fountain pens. It was the same with Maslama, which seemed to be an Arabic word: it was a name for different people and different things. As for Picator, the search engine kept asking her if she meant something else.

It was no help. The three words on their own couldn't give up any information. Obviously they meant something taken together, but what? Sophie had the bright idea of running all three words together on the search engine: but that yielded precisely zero references.

Sophie still had her bedroom PC laptop switched on when her dad came up to kiss her goodnight. 'Come on, sweetie, you've got school in the morning.'

She powered down the computer and got into bed. Her dad kissed her on the forehead. 'I love you, sweetie. Night night. Don't worry about that silly old history test.'

'Okay,' said Sophie. 'Night night.'

7

'I've honestly no idea,' James said. 'None whatso-
ever. The words don't mean anything to me.'

Sophie had been up and ready to intercept James
on his way to school. She'd had to use all her
willpower to prevent herself from leaping on him
like a lioness. She'd blurted it all out to him: the
chamois, the window-cleaning, the words on the
glass.

When he was bewildered, which he was at that
moment, James had a habit of taking off his glasses
and putting them back on again. It was as if he
needed to remind himself that he couldn't see any
clearer without them than he could with them. 'Oh
God, here's your friend again. Quick, change the
subject.'

'Morning, Sophie!' Suki said, swinging her dark
ponytail. 'Morning Jimmy.' Her voice was brittle.

'It's James, actually.'

Suki wasn't having that. 'No no no. Too formal.

If you're going to walk with us plebs every morning it's going to have to be Jimmy.'

'Did I say you were plebs?' James protested.

'Did I say that you said we were plebs?' Suki retorted.

'Cut it out, you two,' Sophie said.

'Anyway,' Suki said, 'Amy and I are going to that place we mentioned tonight. And we've decided you can even bring Jimmy boy here along with you if you really, really have to.'

James looked at Sophie and said, 'Er, by the way, Mrs Royston said yes.'

'She did?' said Sophie.

'Who the heck is Mrs Royston?' Suki wanted to know.

'Yes. Tonight. After school.'

'Who is Mrs Royston?'

'Really? Tonight? Good. Good. That's good news.' For Sophie it was good news indeed. Even though she'd never met Mrs Royston, it came to her as an enormous relief that someone – anyone – might be able to shine a light on the things that were happening to her lately. The way she was feeling, she would have walked barefoot over hot coals to go to see this Mrs Royston.

'So is someone going to tell me who the heck is this Mrs Royston?' Suki asked for the third time.

Sophie looked at James for help. She couldn't exactly tell Suki the truth: that she had no idea who Mrs Royston was, other than that James had indicated that she was an ancient neighbour who might know things about . . . about what? About shimmers, and hawkers in the night, and leather cloths impregnated with strange words that imprinted themselves on the window. Right.

James just looked back at her, took off his glasses and put them on again. Some help he was.

'She's a lady . . . and she . . .'

'And?' said Suki.

Sophie looked desperately at James. 'She gives extra history lessons,' he said, 'after school.'

Sophie squeezed her eyes shut. James might just as well have said that Mrs Royston staged snail races in her back garden, or offered talks on her collection of toby jugs.

Suki shook her head, as if to loosen the wax in her ears. 'Like, yes.'

'Er, yes,' James said, improvising like mad. 'Sophie wanted some help with her history.'

'I really enjoy,' Suki said, squinting sideways at Amy, 'when someone lies through their front teeth.'

They had arrived at the traffic lights and had to wait amid a swirl of Castle boys and Abby girls before crossing.

'Hey, it's the geek boy!' someone shouted. 'And he's picked up a couple of Abby boilers!'

'Boilers?' Suki said loudly. 'That's a new one. Amy, let's get out of here. These two are giving us a bad rep.'

Sophie turned to James. 'Tonight,' she whispered.

'Can you make a good cup of tea?' was the first thing Mrs Royston said to Sophie. '*He* can't,' meaning James, 'not even to save his life.'

Mrs Royston seemed a little fierce. She was a tiny woman with a huge presence. Her skin was an explosive pink, contrasting with her silver-white hair that she wore in a wave with a big white fringe resting across the top of dark glasses. They weren't like ordinary sunglasses either. The glass in them was especially black and especially thick. What's more, she seemed to wear these dark glasses permanently. Even indoors. She had a stick that she needed to help her getting about, but she looked like she might just swing it as a weapon.

She also seemed to be protected by three huge dogs. James introduced them as Sasha, Tara and Mrs Finny: three abandoned black mongrels that Mrs Royston had re-homed. They leapt towards Sophie immediately and all needed petting before they relaxed and settled down again.

'I think so,' Sophie said, referring to the tea.

'You think so or you know so? Well, we'll see. Don't just stand there, get the kettle on. James will show you where everything is.'

James had brought Sophie to Mrs Royston's house immediately after school. At school Sophie hadn't even had a chance to offer much of an alternative to James's 'history lessons' story. Her two friends were distant, even to the point of avoiding her.

When an opportunity did come along, Sophie had heard herself inventing a load of complete tosh about how her mum and dad had promised James's father that she'd spend more time with him, even if that meant being kind to a neighbour called Mrs Royston, who was almost blind and needed little errands running, so it was hardly something Sophie could refuse.

In fact the bigger and more long-winded this fabrication got the more unbelievable it began to sound in her own ears. When Amy had asked her if it was, in that case, like charitable work, Sophie had said that it was, sort of.

'Good,' Suki had said coldly. 'You run along and do your charity work, then.'

And here she was, making tea for an old lady

who could hardly get about on her own feet, so she felt that there was a grain of truth in the lie she'd told her friends.

'Where are the tea bags?' she said to James. It came out a little crossly. She still hadn't quite forgiven him for making her have to explain a sudden passion for history.

'She doesn't like tea bags. You have to use loose tea and make it in a pot.'

'I've only ever made it with tea bags!'

'Okay, I'll do it. Just say that you made it.'

Her every move in the old lady's kitchen was tracked by the three black dogs. Each dog sat upright, front paws resting before it, pink tongue hanging out, watching her. She felt as if she were on trial, and that the dogs would be her jury.

As the kettle boiled Sophie looked around the small cramped kitchen. The floral wallpaper had faded and was peeling slightly at the edges. There were several photographs in silver frames, mostly showing a woman whom she took to be Mrs Royston in her younger days, but with some pretty strange companions. In one picture the younger Mrs Royston wore khaki trousers and shirt and had her arm round the shoulders of a small tribesman with a bone through his nose. Another picture was taken in the jungle and she stood next to a man with feathers in his hair and wearing a loincloth. They were both smiling, and the man was holding up to the camera what looked like a –

'Yes,' James said, 'it's a shrunken head.'

'What?'

'She's got one in the house. Keeps it in a trunk. She might show it to you.'

'You're joking! I don't want to see it.'

'She lived with cannibals for two years.' James spooned tea into a chipped brown teapot. 'And she can make poison-tipped darts.'

'I'd better keep on her good side, then,' said Sophie.

'Yep. You'd better. Right, now we have to take this through on a tray or she'll just send me back. Cups, saucers, milk, sugar, spoon, tea strainer. Right, let's go.'

Sophie glanced nervously at the three dogs, who were still watching.

Mrs Royston had a small coal fire burning in the hearth, even though it wasn't particularly cold inside or out. The three dogs flopped in front of the fire as if it had been lit for their benefit and no one else's. The living room was like a library in that it was walled on all sides with shelves of books. The floor was of highly polished wood, carpeted with one large oriental tasselled rug, woven with exotic blue and scarlet fibres. More photographs and curious objects cluttered the room. Even the top of the piano in the corner of the room was piled with books and trinkets. The piano lid was open, Sophie noticed, and the ivory keys had turned yellow, not unlike the colour of Mrs Royston's teeth.

A high-winged armchair was drawn up next to the fire, in which the old lady sat back, looking tiny but regal. For just a moment it seemed to Sophie that Mrs Royston looked like the ancient and fading empress of some fabulous and far-off land, sitting in her throne, attended by servants.

'Did you let it stand?' she asked mildly, indicating the teapot.

'Not yet,' Sophie said.

'You have to be very precise about letting it stand, young lady. If it doesn't stand long enough, the tea will be weak; too long, and it will stew and become acidic.'

'Shall I put the milk in the cup before the tea, or after?' Sophie said. She'd heard something about the way the Queen liked to have her tea. She just couldn't remember which way it was.

'I don't give a bloomin' damn, my dear,' said Mrs Royston, 'and neither should you, about things like that. Now then, James, who is this *gel* you've brought me?'

It seemed to Sophie that Mrs Royston was quite a posh person. That is, she spoke with a rather posh accent. Sophie didn't know anyone who said *gel* or *bloomin' damn*. But there was nothing special about this little house she lived in. In fact Sophie lived in a larger house, so she couldn't possibly have been all that posh. Unless, Sophie thought, she was posh once but wasn't now, if that sort of thing was possible.

'Her name is Sophie McQueen,' said James, 'and she sees things on walls that aren't there. Like I do.'

'Are you another *savant*?' Mrs Royston said.

'I'm not sure what one of those is. In fact I'm not sure about much at all.'

'Oh, I think you are,' Mrs Royston said sharply. 'I get a very strong impression about people. I think you are capable of being very sure about a lot of things. Just like I'm sure it's about time you poured that tea.'

Sophie glanced at James, who was busy pulling two hard-backed chairs away from the dining table for them to sit on. They were like antique chairs, made of carved mahogany with battered green velvet cushion seats. Like everything else about Mrs Royston they seemed to belong to another place, another much grander house. Sophie made to pour the tea.

'Stop!' cried Mrs Royston. 'Stir it first, my gel, stir it.' Sophie stirred the tea in the pot before pouring it into the white bone-china cups James had placed on the tray. Mrs Royston blew gently on the tea, more from years of habit than to actually cool it, and took a sip. 'At last! Thank goodness! Someone who knows how to make a good pot of tea! You can't believe what cups of bitterness that boy brings me, Sophie. A *savant*, my dear, is one who knows.'

'Knows what?'

'That I can't tell you. Sadly for me I am not a *savant*. I have a more scientific nature. I'm only a poor anthropologist, who has spent her life at the margins of the world. You know what an anthropologist is?'

Sophie hadn't got a clue.

'Someone who studies humans,' James put in.

'I knew that,' said Sophie.

Mrs Royston smiled. 'James is right. Before I retired I was a university professor. It was my job to travel and study different cultures and societies all round the world. And after fifty years, do you know what I found?'

'Tell me.'

'They're all the same.'

'What?' Sophie said indignantly. 'We don't all wear bones through our noses.'

Mrs Royston laughed. It was a short, high-pitched shriek. 'Quite right, Sophie. But that's just stuff on the surface. Like whether you choose to put your milk in your cup before you pour your tea, or afterwards. Deep down, all human beings are the same. And every single culture I ever visited, lived among, studied or researched all had their *savants*. People who can see things that their family and friends cannot.

'It's also down to the luck of the draw how your family and friends might treat you. On one side of the world, a *savant* might be treated as a god, or near to a god; on the other side of the world a *savant* might be tied in a sack with weights and thrown into a river.' Mrs Royston leaned forward slightly in her chair, and Sophie had the impression she was telling her something very important. 'A *savant* would want to be very careful indeed about whom she talks to about her abilities.'

Sophie felt a tiny wave of fear, sensing a warning in Mrs Royston's voice. She looked at James. He was staring back at her. He simply made a nervous gesture of stroking his hand through his mop of curly hair.

'Now let me tell you this, Sophie. Anything that James has told me over the past, oh, year and a half, has stayed between me and him. I've never passed

74

this information on to anyone else. And I wouldn't dream of doing so. Is that right, James?'

'That's right.'

'There. So it's entirely up to you. While I would counsel silence to be your best friend on these matters, if you choose to tell me anything, it stays in this room. Are there things you want to tell me?'

A coal shifted in the grate. Sophie was aware of two pairs of eyes focused on her. She'd already told James about most of her other experiences, and even though she'd only known Mrs Royston a few minutes she believed her to be honest. Sasha, part collie, lifted her head and looked at Sophie as if also waiting for a reply.

So Sophie told Mrs Royston everything.

While Mrs Royston sipped her tea she told her about the shimmers, and when they'd first started. She told her about how they felt like dreams but that she always knew they were not dreams. She told her about the writing on the wall and about how it had disappeared, and how she had met James and he was the only other person she knew who had seen the graffiti on the wall before it had vanished. Then she recounted the visit of the hawker in the middle of the night, followed by the street hawker who had sold her father the chamois leather; and finally about how the chamois leather had left words etched onto the window glass. She told Mrs Royston what those words were.

Mrs Royston set her bone-china cup and saucer down on the occasional table beside her. '*Ravendale, maslama, picator,*' she said. '*Ravendale, maslama, picator.*'

'Do you know what the words mean?' Sophie asked hopefully.

Mrs Royston shook her head. 'Taken together, no. Individually, they might mean anything. Though let's put the *ravendale* aside for a moment, because that might mean anything. The trouble is, it's ringing too many bells. But *maslama* and *picator*, taken together, can mean the same thing.'

'Which is what?'

'*Maslama* is an Arabic word. Sometimes it is just a name. But it has a meaning, and I think its meaning in this case is exactly the same as the word *picator*, which is not Arabic but Latin. They both mean "one who stings" or "one who pricks".'

Sophie and James exchanged nervous glances.

'But what has this to do with me?' Sophie cried in frustration.

Mrs Royston smiled and put her hands together, prayer fashion, under her chin. 'My dear, it is not I who am the *savant*. It is you and James.'

'But I've no more idea than Sophie,' said James.

'It doesn't mean anything to me either.'

'Does it mean,' Sophie asked, more than a little afraid, 'that something is going to sting me?'

'Or us?' said James.

Mrs Royston blinked from behind her dark glasses. 'Possibly. But I think not. I think the hawker is a helper, not an enemy. I think there's something else going on with these words. You see, there is something interesting. *Maslama* is a feminine form, and *picator* is masculine. A girl and a boy. Where else do we have a girl and a boy?'

Sophie looked at James and James looked at Sophie.

'Exactly,' said Mrs Royston. 'No, and on the contrary, I think it is you two who are being named. You are the ones who sting.'

Sophie went home from Mrs Royston's that evening with a heavy heart. She felt that she'd learned something and nothing at the same time. Regarding the meaning of the names, Mrs Royston admitted that she was only guessing. And as for the word *ravendale*, it didn't suggest anything to her. She'd told Sophie and James that if they thought about it for long enough they would come up with something. But beyond this, she could be of no help.

Mrs Royston had said that she only knew what she had learned in books and through study over the years, whereas they had what she called *insight*.

'But who is sending these messages?' Sophie wanted to know. 'And who is the hawker? And why would they communicate in Latin or Greek?'

'I know you must have a million questions,' Mrs Royston had replied. 'But you have to understand that I can't answer them all. Where I can help, I will, but you will come to know a lot more than I do. In the meantime I advise you that you need to hang on to each other, and be a friend to each other. Believe me, you need each other, even if it's just to convince yourselves that you're not going mad.'

Sophie had looked at James. He didn't seem too pleased at this idea. In fact he'd taken off his glasses and shaken his head when he thought Sophie wasn't looking. Well, Sophie wasn't all that thrilled to be shackled with the Geek. Then she felt mean for thinking such thoughts. She knew that what Mrs Royston was saying was true. The only person she could talk to about her strange visions was some-one who also experienced them. And the only person she knew was James.

'Meanwhile,' Mrs Royston had said, 'my advice is

for you both to be alert for more signs, stay calm and drink tea. And on that note we'll have one more cup and then you two can leave me in peace.'

8

'Dad, does the word *ravendale* mean anything to you?'

'Wha?' Sophie's dad had his feet up on the sofa and was reading a book. Her mum sat across from him, leafing though holiday brochures. Meanwhile the television was broadcasting softly from the corner but no one was paying it any attention.

'*Ravendale.*'

'Uh?'

'You know, for someone whose job is listening with prize ears, you don't hear very much, do you?'

'Pardon?'

This was his regular joke. When anyone accused him of not listening he'd say, 'Pardon?'

'Very funny. What about you, Mum?'

'The Greek islands look nice in spring,' Mum said.

'Ooo wakka jakka oo wakka jakka,' said Sophie.

This made both her parents look up. 'I think your

daughter is a bit odd,' Dad said.

'Finally I've got your attention! *Ravendale!*'

'What about it?' said her mum.

'Does the word mean anything to you?'

'Wasn't there a Ravendale Road when we lived in London?' Mum said.

'No,' said Dad, 'you're thinking of Avondale Road.'

'No, Avondale Road was where your Aunty Flo used to live. I mean the one that ran under the railway arches.'

'That wasn't Ravendale Road. That was Riddledale Road.'

'Are you sure?'

'Sure I'm sure. I'm never wrong.'

'I don't think you're right about this.'

'Well, it wasn't Ravendale Road, that's certain.'

Sophie felt like screaming. 'Oh, I give up,' she said, and left her parents to their books and brochures and unwatched television.

Upstairs in her bedroom she sent a text message to James. It read: *nothing.* They had agreed to keep each other informed about any information they'd managed to dig up. They never actually called each other, since that would mean acknowledging that they were friends, or at least something like friends. Texting was more impersonal and kept things on a business level.

After a few minutes her phone bleeped and a similar message was returned. *Same here.*

The next morning Sophie didn't bother waiting for James since she knew he had a dental appointment.

'Where's the Geek?' Suki asked when she met Sophie at the corner of the road.

'Don't call him that,' Sophie said. 'His name is James.'

Suki made a face at Sophie. 'You know you really should come out with me and Amy.'

'Where is it you go exactly?'

'It's a lot of fun. If you could only tear yourself away from your little friend.'

'So what's the big mystery? You still haven't told me where it is you go!'

'It's no mystery. We go to . . . No. If you want to know, come along. Find out for yourself. You should come with us.'

'Yeh and you should come to judo with me,' said Sophie, knowing perfectly well that she'd asked her friend at least four times before without result.

'Please yourself,' said Suki.

They crossed the washbrook and walked between the trees towards the church in silence. Sophie brooded on how Suki had been sharp with her lately; how she seemed distracted all the time.

As they passed by the derelict farmhouse a kind of sigh issued from the old building. A breeze picked up in the trees and made the DEMOLITION: KEEP OUT sign swing on its last remaining screw.

Sophie had stopped abruptly and was staring at the ruined old brick building.

'What is it?' Suki asked.

Sophie had turned quite white. 'Right . . .' she said. 'Right . . .'

Suki followed the track of Sophie's gaze.

It was the same ruined house that they'd passed by every day to and from their way to school. There seemed nothing unusual about it. The doors and windows were boarded up as they always had been. The roof had collapsed and the tiles had mostly slithered into the attic space, but it had been that way for as long as she could remember. The sorry ruin was just awaiting the bulldozer. The story was that the nearby tennis club had purchased the land and when the house was finally knocked down they were going to lay out one or two new tennis courts. Whatever it was that seemed to have Sophie hypnotised, Suki couldn't see it.

'Sophie. What you looking at?'

Sophie seemed to suddenly recover her awareness. 'I just came over a little dizzy. I'm fine. Let's go.'

It was lunchtime before she sent a text message to James. She had to go into the girls' toilets to send the text, because she knew that Amy and Suki would immediately ask her who she was texting. She waited a while in the toilet cubicle but a text never returned, and neither did a message saying that her text had been received. Both Abby and Castle were strict about mobile phones. They were officially not allowed. If you were seen with a phone it would be confiscated. Even so, many of the girls at Abby and the boys at Castle carried them, like contraband, at the bottom of their school bags. Some teachers would confiscate them immediately; some were more tolerant. Sophie had easily persuaded James to take his in case she needed to text him urgently, and that moment had arrived on the first day following her request.

Sophie left her phone on silent ring amid the clutter at the bottom of her bag. The afternoon dragged. History was like ploughing a muddy field with a team of oxen. Maths was like ploughing a muddy field with a team of dying oxen. RE was like ploughing a muddy field with a team of oxen that had keeled over and lay dead in the mud. Then, at the most quiet moment of the year in the most silent lesson of the day in the sleepiest subject in school, her mobile phone vibrated at the bottom of her bag.

Three times.

In supposedly silent mode it sounded like someone starting up a chainsaw and setting to work on a wet log. It buzzed. It buzzed again. And again. The vibration was even enough to move her school bag three inches across the floor. Sophie closed her eyes.

Mrs Scraptoft, the RE teacher, was a tall woman, as slim as a reed, who always wore a coloured chiffon scarf to hide the veins in her thin neck. Every lesson she smelled like the perfume counter at Boots. With her eyes closed Sophie could smell the perfume advancing slowly her way. When the cloud of perfume was almost overpowering her, Sophie opened her eyes to see Mrs Scraptoft standing over her, hands on hips and sharp elbows pinned back like chicken wings. Mrs Scraptoft was the most pointy person she'd ever seen. Pointy elbows, knees, nose, ears and somehow, impossibly, pointy eyes.

Mrs Scraptoft said nothing. She simply very slowly offered the palm of her hand, fixing Sophie with a baleful stare. Sophie coloured and reached into her bag to find the offending phone. She wanted to see what the return message was, but didn't dare to look. She placed the offending phone in Mrs Scraptoft's waiting palm.

. Mrs Scraptoft also had a very high-pitched voice. 'As you know, I like to give my girls a choice,' she said. 'Lose your phone for a week or take a detention after school tonight. You decide.'

Sophie blinked and chose the detention. It was a tough choice because the detention would go on her record and be mentioned in her school report. But she desperately needed her phone back later that evening in order to contact James.

At the end of the school day, before her detention class, Sophie found Amy and asked her to tell James, if she saw him, that she wouldn't be able to walk back with him. 'Where's Suki, by the way?'

'Don't know.'

'Amy, I've been meaning to ask you: who is that guy she's hanging round with?'

'What guy?'

'You haven't seen him? I think he's quite a bit older than her. Long coat?'

'I've no idea.'

Sophie looked hard at Amy. Amy didn't look as if she was lying. But surely she would know something about Suki's boyfriend. 'Really? You don't know anything about him?'

'Look,' Amy said angrily, '*you're* the one with a

boyfriend. Are you making up stories, Sophie? What exactly are you up to?'

Sophie found James waiting for her in the church graveyard. When she came upon him he had his feet on the bench and was lying back with his eyes closed and his hands folded behind his head. His trouser turn-ups had ridden up his leg a little way, high enough for her to see that he wore one brown sock and one black sock.

She approached him without a sound and stood watching his eyelashes flicker. Perhaps he felt her shadow, because he opened his eyes and on seeing her he sat up immediately.

'How long have you been standing there?' he demanded.

'Half an hour.'

'You lie!'

'I do. About ten seconds.'

'That's creepy.'

'Not as creepy as odd socks.'

James glanced down and crossed his feet at his ankles, as if to hide his mismatching socks. 'Anyway, what's so important?'

'On your feet,' said Sophie, 'and follow me.'

Without looking back to see if he was following, Sophie walked around to the front of the church and out through the lych gate. The lych gate itself gave her a tiny shiver, and always had since she'd heard that it was the place where the bearers at a funeral would pause for the priest to start the service before carrying the dead person onto the hallowed ground. It was like a portal to another world. Sophie always fancied that she could see figures at the corner of her vision, and so she hurried through.

Out of the church grounds she took the path towards the washbrook, and then the path towards the tennis club. When she drew abreast of the old ruined house she stopped and turned her gaze towards the door.

'What?' James wanted to know. 'What is it?'

Sophie said nothing. She wanted to see if James would see the thing for himself.

It wasn't that she wanted to be mysterious. She wanted to study his reaction. Because when she'd seen the thing that morning, a tiny charge of electricity had surged through her body. She wanted to be sure that James felt the same thing as she did; that this was not just some wild coincidence.

'What am I supposed to be looking at?' James spluttered.

Sophie just shook her head.

Then James looked back at the door of the

boarded, derelict house and he spotted it. Sophie knew he'd spotted it because he hugged himself, as if he'd suddenly been chilled. He looked at her. She nodded.

Then James went tearing across the grass towards the house and stood right under the entrance, looking up at the lintel stone above the door arch.

Chiselled into the red brickwork and almost blackened with age was the word *Ravendale*.

'How many times have we walked past it?' James said. 'How many times?'

'It's not a coincidence, is it?' Sophie wanted reassuring.

'No way. How did you spot it?'

'This morning. I'd like to say it was nothing. But a wind blew and made the board flap. It was almost as if something was directing my attention here.'

James stepped over to the DEMOLITION: KEEP OUT board. It was hanging by a single screw. He moved it with his hand. It swung back into place. 'Pretty stiff,' he said.

'Doesn't matter. Doesn't matter, because we're going to have to go inside, aren't we?'

'Yeh, right!' James said, too loudly, meaning: *are you completely insane?*

'So, we've taken all this time to figure out what

Ravendale was, and now we've found it, you're just going to walk away?'

'You think we should go in there? You're nuts. It's about to fall down.'

'It's been there for three hundred years or more. I don't think it's going to fall down just yet.'

'Well, count me out. I'd rather stick my head in a fish-tank full of biting piranhas. In fact I'd rather stick my toes in the bread-slicer than go wandering around that wreck. In fact I'd rather –'

'You're scared,' said Sophie.

'Too right I'm scared. And so would any sensible person be. Have you noticed what people do in an earthquake? They run away from falling buildings. It's called using your intelligence. I mean, just look at it! It might collapse at any moment!'

'That's not what you're afraid of, James.'

'What?'

'It's not that the building might fall, is it?'

James held his head and groaned softly. 'No.'

Sophie turned back to study the building. Under the collapsed roof the red-brick walls seemed sturdy enough. But the house had a sour air about it, probably caused by years of neglect. She thought it must have been a very fine house once. She imagined people sitting around a table, maybe for Christmas dinner a hundred years ago. And for an eerie moment she thought she heard music coming from one of the rooms.

The sound was like fiddle music, the distant burst of a reel. It should have been a happy sound, but it ran through Sophie like a sword, piercing her with notes that spoke of sadness and pain and of being locked away. But just as suddenly the fiddle stopped and the music disappeared. Sophie thought it must have been caused by the strength of her imagination alone. But then she looked at James.

'Did you hear that?' she asked him.

'Fiddle music? Lonely and cold?'

She nodded, and he shivered. Sophie understood that it was not her imagination after all; or if it was, then it was an imagination she and James shared. 'Let's try round the back.'

'Wait,' said James.

Some Year Ten stragglers from Sophie's school were approaching the washbrook. If James and Sophie were spotted sneaking behind the old house, that would be it. Everyone in both schools would know within twenty-four hours that they had been seen snogging. Sophie didn't like that idea any more than James did, so they pretended to be comparing their maths homework as the school stragglers passed by. It occurred to Sophie that she would now be thought of as a geek. Well, it was either a geek or an easy snogger.

'Okay, let's be quick,' said James, stepping over a pile of rubble and moving hurriedly towards the back of the house. But this time it was Sophie's turn to stop them. She'd spotted the high-visibility jackets of two police community officers on patrol and moving towards them.

'This is hopeless,' she said. 'There are too many people around. We'll have to come back tonight.'

'What? I'm not going in there in the dark!' James wailed.

The idea didn't appeal to Sophie any more than it did to James. 'Okay. It starts getting dark around seven. When it's dusk, I mean. There should be enough light to see by but the dusk will give us a bit of cover if we're snooping around.'

James still didn't seem too happy. But as he looked up, the police officers were heading towards them. 'Come on,' he said. 'Let's go.'

She returned with the dusk settling gently first amongst the leaves of the trees, then on the shoulders of the church, and finally on the broken roof of the house. Sophie thought James might not be coming, but then she saw the swinging motion of his steady progress towards her.

'What you got there?'

He produced a small crowbar and a hammer from under his coat. 'Well, if we're going to go in we've got to get inside somehow.'

'Is that going to be necessary?'

'Well, even if there is a bell and you ring it, I can't imagine someone answering to let us in. Can you?'

'All right, funny-arse! No need to be sarcastic.'

'Well then,' James said, 'use your sense.'

Sophie had to bite her lips to prevent herself from saying any more. Instead she made long strides towards the back of the house, not even checking to see if he was following.

Just as they were at the front of the house, the windows were all boarded up. There were a couple of crumbling outbuildings: a toilet and a coal-house. These gave way to the back door itself, which had been blocked by a steel shutter. Over the years the builders had used stronger and stronger measures to stop people breaking into the deserted building. Now it looked like it might be easier to break into a bank.

'This isn't going to be easy,' Sophie said.

The outbuildings were joined to the house by a tiny flat roof, and just above it was a small window boarded by a wooden panel. 'Give me a foot up,' said James.

Sophie interlaced her fingers and held her hands

so that James could place the sole of one shoe over her palms. 'Ow!' cried Sophie.

'Okay, you go instead.'

'No, I'm okay. It's just . . . Ow!'

James kicked off and scrambled up onto the square of flat roof. He lay on his stomach and reached down to help Sophie up.

'I'll stay here and keep a lookout,' said Sophie.

'No, you bloody well won't! Get up here with me! You were the one who insisted on coming here, right?'

It was true. But now they were there, Sophie was beginning to have big doubts. The fear of getting caught was bad enough. But now she was starting to wonder what she would find inside the house: what it was that seemed to have been calling both her and James. What was even more stupid was that neither of them had told anyone where they were going. If anything happened, they might never be found. Her stomach squeezed at the thought.

The dusk was gathering around them. If they waited much longer they would have to go inside in darkness. Sophie reached up to grab James's outstretched hand and, with a struggle, managed to clamber up on to the flat roof beside James.

'So far so good,' he said.

The plywood boarding the window was itself

quite old. The rain and the sun had softened it. When James stuck his crowbar behind, the board simply popped over the nails holding it to the window frame. It pulled back easily, opening up wide enough for them to climb in.

'Not such a geek, are you?' Sophie said.

'Thanks. Any more insults, or are we going in?'

James went to go first but there was a problem. The window was a light-well onto a flight of stairs. He could just about make out the steps below him in the darkness. He dropped down and landed safely before calling to Sophie to follow him.

Sophie didn't land so easily. Expecting a longer drop, she lost her footing on the stairs and rolled into a wall. 'Ooof!' she cried.

'Never mind ooof, get up,' said James.

'I hadn't realised it would be so dark in here, what with everything boarded up,' Sophie said, rubbing her ankle.

'Did you think to bring a torch?' hissed James.

'No. Did you?'

'Hey, I brought the crowbar! Am I supposed to think of everything?' He flashed a powerful light in Sophie's eyes. 'Lucky for you one of us has got some brains around here.'

They stood in stillness for a moment, trying to get a sense of the house. There was an overwhelming reek of damp and neglect. Beyond that there was not a sound. From inside the boarded house they could barely even hear the sound of traffic near by. The house existed in another world. It was like a cold, damp tomb.

They had dropped onto a landing where the stairs turned to go up and down. James flashed his torch up the stairway leading to the bedrooms and then down the stairs leading to the rest of the house. 'Up or down?' he said. 'You choose.'

'Do we have to?' said Sophie.

'No,' James said. 'We don't have to. We could get out of here right away. We could ignore everything that told us to come here. The hawker. Ravendale. All of that. Nothing is making us stay here. We could just forget all about it.'

Sophie sighed, and her sigh seemed to wing around the damp walls of the house, like a bird trying to find its way out. Her skin flushed cold. Her mouth was so dry that her tongue stuck to the roof of her mouth. She wanted to free her tongue, to say something to James, but she was even afraid of the sound she would make. The pair of them stood on the landing, not knowing what to do.

'Do you smell anything unusual?' James whispered.

Sophie twitched her nose. 'Just awful damp.'

James shone his torch up the stairs, and Sophie took that as a sign that she should go up. Her legs had turned to slush. She could barely put one foot in front of the other. But she took one small step, then another. James followed, shining the torch in front of her.

At the front of the house the bedroom doors stood ajar, and the dusky blue light from outside shone through the broken roof and lit up the bedrooms. The floors were littered with plaster and wooden laths and tiles from the broken roof. James shone his torch into the corners of the room but there was nothing. The rooms at the back also showed that the house had been stripped of everything long ago. The only thing remaining was the yellow wallpaper.

'Come on,' said James, and he turned his torch back to the stairs.

Downstairs was the same. From what was the dining room, even the fire surround had been removed from the large open fireplace. In the kitchen, all cupboards and work surfaces had been lifted out. There was nothing in the way of furniture, decoration, or any kind of object. Just the shell of the house remained. The shell and its shadows.

'It just feels so sad,' Sophie said.

'The house?' asked James. 'Or something in it?'

'I don't know.'

Sophie looked back. Her eyes were becoming accustomed to the dark and it seemed like a soft blue light, maybe still pouring in through the roof, was making it slightly easier to see. It was an odd blue illumination: one that pulsed quite slowly; or perhaps it was her beating heart that created the effect.

'I really don't see anything,' said James. 'If we've been brought here, then it's for nothing. I don't know what I expected to find, but there's nothing here.'

Their terror of the house was subsiding now. They made a thorough search, shining the torch into the space under the stairs, peering into the fireplaces, but nothing came to light. They made another search of the bedrooms, as far as they could, because the upstairs floorboards felt rotten and none too safe. Finding nothing of interest they returned downstairs, discovering another small room at the back of the house.

'Someone has been here,' James whispered.

He shone his torch on an old mattress in the corner. The room was dry and scattered around the mattress were wine and beer bottles and cans. There were ashtrays spilling with cigarette butts.

'It looks recent,' James said. 'Could be kids from

school coming in here.'

But Sophie didn't answer. Her hands were covering her ears as if she was blocking out some loud noise. She had a picture in her mind. But the picture was like that seen reflected in water and disturbed by ripples. The picture wouldn't fix, but what she thought she saw was a young girl with dark ringlets of hair, and she was locked in a room with barred windows; and she was crying. There came a momentary burst of that same fiddle music; and in that moment the picture dissolved and translated to an overwhelming feeling of sadness and despair that made Sophie want to cry, too.

'I don't like what I'm feeling here, James. Can we get out?'

'Yeh. I've had enough of it.'

Sophie went first, and it wasn't too difficult to scramble onto the windowsill where they'd come in. James followed her out, replacing the jemmied board as best he could, before dropping off the flat roof to join Sophie. By now the dusk had given way to night and a moonless black sky, leading Sophie to wonder where the blue light inside the house had come from.

'Back to square one,' said James.

Sophie was about to agree when she heard it again: that same snatch of faraway fiddle music. It lasted for no longer than two or three notes, and yet it drew her attention to the outhouses, where she thought she saw a tiny pulse of blue light.

'What is it?' James wanted to know.

'Did you hear it? The music again?'

James shook his head. He'd heard nothing.

'Bring your torch.'

Sophie stepped over to the outhouses. There were two wooden doors. Leprous paint was peeling from the doors, and the latch on the first one Sophie tried was rusted shut. At last it popped open to reveal a dry toilet minus its seat. She closed the door and tried the other one. The second door opened more easily, but something obstructed it. She put her shoulder to it but it wouldn't budge.

'What's blocking it?' James said. 'Hope it's not a body.'

Sophie gave him an evil look. 'Come on, help me shove it open.'

Together they managed to shove the door open far enough for James to get one arm through and shove his way in. He flashed his torch at the object obstructing them. He managed to drag it back from the door, so that Sophie could see it.

'It's just a box of rotten old books,' said James, sorting through the grimy, soggy paperbacks and mildewed hardbacks stacked in a huge cardboard box. 'What's this? *From Russia With Love*. More like *From Russia With Slug*.' A large and bloated rust-coloured slug clung to the dirty cover of the book. James chucked it aside. He held up another book. '*The Miraculous Birth of Language*. Gosh, that looks old.' It was so old and damp the cover practically crumpled under his fingers.

'Is there nothing else there?' Sophie wanted to know.

'Nope. Just a load of soggy old books.' James lifted out a pile of the books but couldn't hold on to them, and they slipped from his grasp, littering the cement floor of the outhouse building. 'Hello, what's this one?'

'What is it?' Sophie said, squeezing in next to him.

James had his torch beam angled on another large and very old book. The front cover looked as though it had been torn off, but the binding and the back cover were leather: a dark, crimson leather. Otherwise it looked like a bible, with gold-leaf edges to the paper and gold lettering on the spine.

James shone his torch. *Index Phasmatis et Daemn*.

'Is it Latin?' Sophie asked.

'Yes.'

'Well?'

'Well what?'

'What's it mean?'

'I don't know.'

'But I thought you did Latin at your fancy posh school. What's the point if you can't read simple words?'

'Shaddup and hold the torch.'

Sophie shone the torch on the book as James flicked through it. It seemed to be all kinds of lists, but occasionally there were beautiful colour plates or black-and-white plates of elaborate drawings of the strangest looking creatures and odd designs.

'This is really old,' said James. 'I'm going to keep it for my Black Library.'

'I have a strange feeling,' Sophie said, 'that we were meant to find it.'

James switched off his torch. 'Time to go.'

9

'What a wonderful cup of tea you do make, Sophie!' Mrs Royston peered at Sophie from behind her dark glasses. 'In future you must always make the tea because James couldn't make it to save his life. James, you can be the biscuit monitor.'

James rolled his eyes and went into the kitchen to fetch the biscuit tin full of broken ginger snaps and garibaldis. The three black dogs followed him out, hoping that he was going out for a walk. But the pair had come to tell Mrs Royston of their disappointment at the house. They'd also brought the book that James had found, to see if she could make sense of it; but she refused to look at it until the tea was made.

Sophie had asked her mum how to make a really good pot of tea. It turned out there were a few tricks. First, warm the pot with boiling water to keep the heat in, her mother had told her. Empty it, re-boil the kettle and take the pot to the kettle, not the other way round. One large spoon of tea per person and one for the pot. Stir the tea, replace the lid on the pot. Pour too quickly and the tea is weak; pour too late and the tea is stewed. How long should you leave it to stand? Use your common sense, her mother had said.

Well, her common sense seemed to do the trick on this occasion, because Mrs Royston put her stick aside, sipped from the cup and declared herself delighted with the results. Sophie was concerned with the behaviour of the dogs. They seemed to be very attentive towards her, watching her quietly, yawning and stretching occasionally but always observant. They watched Sophie far more than they watched James or Mrs Royston. Sophie wondered what that meant. They were very placid animals, but Sophie thought how it might be very bad to get on the wrong side of them. It struck her that these dogs would not only be good in a fight, but they might even enjoy one. Sasha in particular had a whiff of wolf about her.

'Biscuits, please,' said Mrs Royston, and when she'd nibbled a garibaldi she listened to what they'd had to say about their visit to Ravendale.

'I have no doubt,' she said, 'that it was the Ravendale in question.'

'But there was nothing there! We searched every

creepy room!' Sophie protested.

'So you say. But you were given an inspirational message to go into that house. And go you did. You can do no more.'

'But what was the point?' James protested.

Mrs Royston took another sip of tea, savouring before swallowing. 'The point? I'm afraid we're dealing with very mysterious forces. What did you expect, James? To be tipped off about the winner of this year's Grand National horse race? To find a sack of gold coins buried under the fireplace?'

'Now you're being sarcastic,' James retorted.

'Indeed I am.' Mrs Royston looked over the rim of her cup at Sophie and beamed her a smile. 'Have you told me everything?'

'Yes,' said James.

'No,' said Sophie. 'There was music. And a blue light.'

'A-ha! Important information. Music and lights.'

'Well,' Sophie said, looking uncertainly at James, 'it was so faint it was barely there. James heard it, too, or he did some of the time. It was fiddle music, at least I think it was, but you only heard a couple of notes before the sound was snatched away.'

'I see. And what about the lights?'

'I heard the music but I didn't see any lights,' James said.

'Don't worry about that. You may find that you are sensitive to different things. Maybe that's why you've been put together.'

James winced. He looked like he disliked the idea of being put together with anyone. 'What do you mean?'

'Well, it's pretty obvious: you're a team. Sounds like you did a pretty good job getting in and out of that house. Anyway, James, stop interrupting. I want to hear about these blue lights.'

'It was not so much lights,' Sophie said, 'as one soft light that seemed to be all over the house. Blue, or even violet. At first I thought it might be coming into the house from outside – you know, from the roof – but then I realised it couldn't be. It seemed to be coming from the house itself.'

'Interesting. Go on.'

'There's no more to tell. Except to say that when the light was there I felt this deep sense of sadness.'

'And then the light went away?'

'Yes. Oh, and then I saw it again later. Very briefly. Flickering from the outhouse.'

'This was where you found James's book?'

'Yes.'

Mrs Royston put down her cup and saucer and removed her sunglasses for the first time. Her eyes were a very pale grey-blue, almost washed out. She

raised her right arm high in the air and then low-
ered her hand over her face, closing her eyelids with
finger and thumb of her right hand. She stayed that
way as if deep in thought. The way in which she
screwed up her face made it look as if this deep
thinking was painful. Sophie looked at James, but
he simply shrugged.

They waited for her to say something important.
She stayed in that strange position for a long time.
Sophie shuffled in her seat. James raked his hand
through his curly hair, looked at his fingernails,
looked out of the window, then looked at his fingernails again. The silver clock on the mantelpiece ticked
loudly, so much that it seemed to fill the room. Sophie
thought Mrs Royston had fallen asleep.

Then a coal shifted in the fire. Mrs Royston lifted
her hand from her eyes and put her dark glasses
back on again. Her lips twitched, as if she was thinking very carefully about what to say. Finally she
asked them, 'Do you want another biscuit?'

'No thanks,' said James.

'I've had enough,' said Sophie.

'Let's have a look,' said Mrs Royston, 'at this
book of yours.'

James had brought the book along in an old
leather satchel. He lifted it out and handed it to Mrs
Royston.

'It's a big brute, isn't it? And it smells pretty bad. I think the paper is very old. It's lost its front cover, I see.' She turned the book sidewise to scrutinise the index. '*Index Phasmatis et Daemn*. Fascinating.'

'It's about demons, isn't it?' said James.

'Not exactly,' said Mrs Royston, carefully turning the pages. 'The word *Daemn* in Latin meant spirits rather than demons. *Phasmatis* meant ghosts. *Index* doesn't mean quite the same as the way that we use it: index is a pointer, as in your index finger. So we might translate the title as "A Pointer to Ghosts and Spirits". Or as the author, who certainly didn't write it in ancient times, might have wanted it: "An Introduction to Ghosts and Spirits". And it certainly has some very saucy illustrations, doesn't it?'

'Why is it written in different languages?' James wanted to know.

'It's a taxonomy, so far as I can see.'

'Duh?'

'A catalogue of ghosts and spirits. Each different spirit – and it looks like it runs to hundreds – has its own brief entry; and each entry is written in Latin, French and English. It's a shame that the front pages have been torn off with the cover, because they are the only pages that might be able to tell us when it was first published. Judging by the style of the language and the print I'd say early nineteenth century, possibly earlier.'

'You mean it's two hundred years old?'

'Could be. Or it could be a copy of a book that old, or even older. Can't say for certain. My goodness, these pages really do smell musty!'

Mrs Royston got out of her chair by the fire and placed the book on the table. Sophie and James pulled up chairs either side of her as she leafed through the book. Some of the pages were damp and stuck together, but she was very careful in separating them so that they were not damaged.

The *Index* was organised like an encyclopaedia. The author of the book said that there were many hundreds – and many different types – of spirits, ghosts, phantoms and apparitions. As far he knew, the author had written, this book was the first ever to try to classify them and list them. Some he said were 'friendly and helpful demons', some were mischievous and some were 'outright malignant'. He hoped that this *Index* would be useful to the enquirer who needed help and guidance in deciding which was which. He finished his introduction with a warning. The spirit world, he said, was not visible to everyone. But no one should be in any doubt that the spirit world existed in reality and was capable of influencing peoples' lives for good or for evil.

Some of the entries had drawings next to them. Most of the illustrations were more like diagrams or geometric shapes than figures, though a few rare drawings did represent the spirits as half-human, half-animal.

The entries themselves were not exactly easy reading. The print was small and the language was very odd and written in a dull and repetitive style. You practically needed a magnifying glass to read it. Each page had three or four entries, and the entries themselves could be counted in the hundreds.

'This is a *very strange* book,' said Mrs Royston. 'You say you found it in the outhouse?'

'Yes,' James said, 'it was an old coal-house. Someone had dumped a box of books there.'

'What other books were there?'

'Just perfectly ordinary old paperbacks. James Bond and stuff like that.'

Mrs Royston sat upright in her chair. 'Well, what a pair of blockheads you both are!'

'What?' James and Sophie said together.

'You said your visit to the house was a waste of time!'

'So it was.'

'Oh no. On the contrary. Whatever it was that drew you to the house had a very clear reason. And this is it. Whatever drew you to the house wanted you to come into possession of this book.'

Sophie and James looked down at the damp, battered, mildew-speckled, foul-smelling old volume on the table before them as if it had suddenly grown a set of teeth.

'My advice to you both is to study it and to take great care of it. Now then: is anyone ready for another cup of tea?'

After James and Sophie had gone, Mrs Royston huddled by the fire, gripping the arms of her chair. The three dogs lay near by, but of the three, Sasha seemed agitated. She sat up, staring hard at Mrs Royston.

'Don't you look at me like that,' said Mrs Royston. 'Anyway, it's not your business.'

Sasha blinked and yawned and continued to stare at the old woman. A coal shifted in the fire. Mrs Royston leaned over to grab a blackened poker, which she used to stab at the burning coals. Then she set the poker down again.

She turned back to the dog. 'If I want to lie to children that's my affair and nothing to do with you. Children have to be lied to. On occasion. Anyway, what would you know about it? You're a dog.'

Sasha opened her jaws and let out a little whine.

The old woman raised her stick at Sasha. 'Stop looking at me like that!'

The dog dropped its head submissively. It lay back down on the rug, accepting its place with the other two dogs. Mrs Royston had never used her stick on the dogs. But just like James and Sophie, the dogs always had the sense that she might.

Mrs Royston took off her dark glasses again. She leaned forward in her chair, her hand holding her eyes shut.

She seemed to be listening. Now all three dogs watched her from their place on the rug.

Mrs Royston knew she would have to let the roaring wind into her house. She had lied to the children. She had her reasons. She hadn't wanted to make things easy for them. And anyway, her special ability was different from theirs. And it hurt.

She too was a *savant*. But she had learned over the years to keep quiet about it. She had never entirely understood her own gift, and never entirely welcomed it. She was afraid that if she'd told the children that she too was like them, that she too had a special capacity to see things that others couldn't, then they would think it was all too common; that lots of people had this gift. But Mrs Royston knew the dangers. She knew the importance of throwing a veil over her peculiar talents. People could be cruel when they knew someone was different.

Mrs Royston discovered her talent when she was on a research field trip, studying a remote tribe in the Amazon jungle. A village witch doctor had given her a potion to drink. It knocked her flat out. It was only when she woke up a day later that she realised that a mask had been ripped off the world.

At certain times a kind of storm would build up before her eyes, and then a rip would appear in the world, like a rent in an artist's canvas. Through the gap she could see the chaotic figures of a world behind this one, bathed in a blazing silver light. At first this sensation was rare and might happen only once or twice a year. Then it began to become more frequent, until the storm before her eyes became a regular thing. What's more, it wasn't always a pleasant experience. It could come as a terrible migraine: a procession of bright colours followed by a crippling headache.

Because the silver light hurt her eyes, she had found by accident that she could make the visions go away just by wearing sunglasses. The glasses acted as a switch. But gradually over the years she found that she needed thicker and darker glass in the lenses to be able to switch off the swirling forms that danced before her. Finally she had to wear the dark glasses all the time, just to be able to get on with her life.

Now, whenever she removed her dark glasses, the storm of light returned, the rent in the canvas reappeared and the world as we see it peeled back to reveal another world behind it, luminous, blinding, terrifying.

And full of creatures, faces, shapes, forms and spirits who wanted to talk with her.

As they walked home, James asked Sophie what they were going to do. Mrs Royston had suggested that they scour the book for anything that might relate to either blue light or even the hawker. She was convinced that it was no accident that they had discovered the *Index*. In fact she was adamant that was why they'd been drawn to the house. Something had wanted them to find it.

The thought made Sophie uneasy. As they walked the streets it made her feel like she might be being watched at all times; by what or by whom she couldn't say. But it made her think of unseen things flying at her shoulder.

'We could spend tomorrow evening going through the book,' James said.

Sophie was almost relieved to remember that she was busy next evening. 'Can't. I've got my judo class.'

'Skip it for once.'

'No. I never skip it. For one thing I love going, and for another thing I want to be good at it.' This was all true; but another thing was that Sophie felt clear and safe with judo. These things that were happening to her, the hawker, the messages, the house, the book, they all seemed to happen in a scary world of shadow. Judo worked in a world of light and certainty, and right now she wanted to hang on to that. She thought James needed it, too. 'Why don't you come?'

'Let's not go into that again.'

'No, really. You'd be good. And it makes you strong-minded.'

'Eh? What are you saying? That I'm weak-minded? Well, I'm already very strong-minded, thanks very much.'

'I don't know why, but I think it will be a help to us. In what we're doing . . .' Sophie didn't really know what she was saying. She felt muddled. But she wanted James to join her for the judo class.

'What's one thing got to do with the other? Anyway, I can't afford it.'

'Can't afford it? It's like two pounds a session. Who can't afford that?' Sophie mocked.

'Well, if you must know,' James said angrily, 'we can't afford it. My dad has been ill and out of work and we have to save every penny.'

Sophie felt confused. 'So, how do you pay the fees for Castle if you're broke? I've heard it costs –'

'I'm there as a favour. I got a part scholarship and the Head is an old friend of my dad's. Satisfied?'

Now Sophie felt mean for teasing him. 'Sorry, I didn't think –'

'No, no one thinks. Everyone assumes if you go to private school you're loaded. Except of course for some of the other kids in the school who know I'm there as a kind of favour and who give me hell for it every sodding day.'

'Phew! Sorry. I mean it.'

James looked utterly miserable. 'Right.'

'Look,' Sophie said brightly, 'it's not a lot. My teacher lets people try out the first couple of sessions free to see if they like it.'

'And if I like it? Yeh? If I really love it, then it will be another thing I can't do, right? Where's the sense in that?'

'Okay, but say you did like it . . . well, it's not a lot and I'd even be prepared to pay for you myself for a couple of sessions until we could work something out.'

'Thanks, Sophie! More charity! Another class where all the other kids will laugh behind my back because I can't afford anything. You really know what a boy wants, don't you?'

Sophie felt bewildered. Every suggestion she made, every offer of help, James seemed to turn into some kind of an insult. Behind his glasses his eyes were swimming with fury.

'James, I was trying to help.'

'Yeh? Well, don't. Because people who are never short of money have no idea what it's like not to have two pennies to rub together. No idea. I'm going.'

Clutching the *Index* under his arm, James turned on his heels and marched away. Sophie was so surprised by his outburst that she didn't even try to call him back. She stood knitting her brows and watching him go.

Sophie walked home deep in thought. James was right in one thing: she had assumed that because he went to Castle school that his dad must be loaded. She suspected that some people pretended to send their kids to private school to get a better education, when the truth was it was to keep their kids from mixing with boys and girls like her. And James had got the worse end of the deal: he was one of the kids that those classmates weren't supposed to mix with, and they knew it. She could guess how miserable his days at Castle might be. It occurred to her that he didn't have a single friend at Castle. And that if he did have a friend at all, then it was her.

So she was relieved when she got a text message from James that evening. *Sorry*, it said. *Would love to come to judo. Can I still?*

10

'The reason why judo means *the subtle way*,' William Trafford explained to James, 'is because it differs from every other form of combat in one special way. It uses the force and speed and strength of an opponent against him.' He looked at Sophie and winked. 'Or *her*. Which is why, with dedication and practice, someone of Sophie's size could easily throw or trip someone of my size and weight.'

James nodded, but he didn't quite believe it. Judo master William was a pretty scary-looking bloke. He was six feet tall in his bare feet, with powerful shoulders and that intimidating squint in one eye. Plus his judo suit exposed a mass of grey chest-hair that looked like the stuffing from an exploded old sofa. Though Sophie said he was kind, he certainly didn't look it. In fact he looked kind of mean.

William smiled and looked at Sophie. 'Your friend doesn't believe me,' he said.

'What?' James protested. 'I didn't say anything!'

'You didn't have to,' William said. 'Judo also teaches us to read body language. People always give away what they might be thinking, but without even speaking. Stand up and Sophie will demonstrate.'

'Will it hurt?' James said doubtfully.

All around him boys, girls and adults were grappling with each other and slamming each other on the floor. Each time someone went down on the mat there was a huge bump and often a groan. It didn't exactly correspond with his idea of fun.

There had been a lot to learn even before walking into the gym where the judo took place. Or rather, walking into the dojo, as Sophie insisted on calling it. It seemed more like a blooming temple than a gym. You had to take your shoes off before going onto the mat and you had to bow to the senior member of the club. James felt a bit of a drip. He was the only person not in a white judo suit. Sophie told him that T-shirt and tracksuit would be fine until he decided if he wanted to carry on coming to the club.

Plus scraping and bowing to people he didn't know made him go red in the face. He had to address William as 'sensei', and he kept forgetting. William never seemed to mind, and never corrected him, but Sophie had warned him that one member of the group, a short, stocky, bearded man called Luke, would shout at him if he heard. Luke had a shaved head. His job was to be a bulldog and to remind everyone of dojo rules and etiquette. Sophie told him if he was shouted at he was supposed to say, 'Thank you, sensei Luke' for being shouted at.

James wasn't at all sure about judo.

'Will it hurt?' William said. 'Stand up and we'll see. Sophie is going to demonstrate on you.'

James shuffled onto the mat.

'I want you to squat down.'

James did as instructed.

'Now Sophie is going to stand in front of you and try to push you back with one hand on your forehead. All you have to do is to move forward.'

Sophie stepped in front of James and placed the flat of her hand on his brow. She dropped her shoulders and set herself to resist him.

'Now,' said William, 'push.'

James leaned forward and put all his strength into pushing Sophie back. She in turn dug her heels in and tried to stop him with her one hand. James was surprised to see that he could make forward progress and that it was taking all of Sophie's powers to hold him back with her one hand. He had thought there was going to be some trick where he wouldn't be able to move forward at all, but he had Sophie retreating a few inches at a time.

'Stop!' shouted William. 'Good. Now try the same thing again, James, but Sophie is going to hold you back with two fingers only.'

James squatted again. This time Sophie stepped to the side of him. She reached from above his nose and placed two fingers lightly under his nostrils. James couldn't see how Sophie could possibly stop him this time. She wasn't in front of him and she wasn't using the flat of her hand.

'Okay,' William shouted. 'Push!'

James pushed forward again, but Sophie simply flipped his nose upwards with her two fingers so that his head was tilted back slightly. He was astonished. He couldn't go forward an inch. In fact the harder he pushed the more he seemed to tilt backwards. He put more strength into his push but all that happened was that his nose started to hurt and he found himself in danger of toppling over on his back.

'You're not trying!' William said with a big smile on his lips and a twinkle in his squinting eye. 'Give it some!'

James steeled himself and pushed forward. It was hopeless. It hurt his nose even more and the greater the energy he put into trying to go forward the higher his head went backwards.

'Enough,' William said, and Sophie stepped smartly backwards. 'I hope you get the point, James. Stand in the right place at the right moment and you could even stop a raging bull. Is your nose okay?'

'Yes,' James said. He looked over at Sophie and saw she was trying to stop herself from laughing.

'Ready to learn some judo?'

'Yes, sensei.'

'Very good. Now judo is not exactly for the faint-hearted. You have to get used to being thrown about, so the first thing we teach you is how to break your fall. Ready?'

'It gets kind of addictive,' Sophie said to James as they were walking back from his first judo class. 'All the things they show you – it really works.'

'Yes, but you couldn't really throw William, could you?'

'No I couldn't. But that's because he's a master. He's ready for it and he sees it coming way ahead. But if it was someone who didn't know the first thing about judo, then I could take them by surprise and put them on the ground before they realised what was happening. Even someone as big and strong as William.'

James rubbed his chin.

Sophie could see what he was thinking. 'Look, James, don't run away with the idea that after a few judo lessons you'll be able to deck all your bullies, 'cos you won't. It takes a lot of practice and you have to stick with it.'

'I want to. I enjoyed it tonight. In fact it was the most fun I've had in . . .' James was going to say that it was the most fun he'd had in his entire life, but he thought it made him sound wet. 'Well, in ages.'

'Great. So you'll come next week?'

'I'm still worried about the dosh, Sophie.'

'We'll sort the money out. I'll help. I promise.'

James looked hard at her, then looked away.

'What?' said Sophie.

'Nothing.'

'What?'

'I just wondered why you're being so kind to me.'

Sophie thought about it. It didn't occur to her that she was being kind. She just did whatever came naturally. 'If you had a choice between being a mean person or a kind person, what would you be?'

'Mean,' said James.

'Really?'

'No, not really at all. Kind. It's just that I'm more

used to people being mean to me rather than kind.'

'Well, maybe you've just been hanging out with the wrong people.'

'Maybe I have.'

11

James had been scouring the *Index*, and something had turned up. He had found it under a section headed 'Lux Lumen Varius'. Mrs Royston had gone through the headings with them and told them that this meant something like 'Various Clear Lights' and thought that it would be a good place to start. The *Index* catalogued what it claimed were well over two thousand different types of spirits, ghosts and demons, and there were about a hundred and fifty entries – not all in English – under this category alone.

The *Index* was written in a curious style, with odd spellings and abbreviations and dots and dashes everywhere, but it was possible to make out a reference to something very much resembling Sophie's experience at the house.

Illuminations of a turquoise or sapphire hue in motion . . . and of an airborne or playful disposition do manifest a relese or appeal esp. for those spiritum of a childish or juvenile propens. And often in distress for want of relese esp. in conjunction with & etc, musicality, festivality & etc.

'Would that fit with the lights you saw inside and around the house?' James asked Sophie.

They were sitting in the churchyard after school. A light breeze stirred the trees around them and the rays of a lovely golden sun turned the stone church tower a warm colour. Even some of the gravestones seemed golden. It seemed a long way from any talk of spirits or ghosts, and from the dark interior of the house that, just fifty or sixty yards away, loomed over their shoulders.

'Could be. What does it say about music?'

'Well, that's just it. I saw that thing about music, so I looked up another section about spirits connected with music. Took me ages to find it then I tripped over a whole section on Acoustics. There are loads of spirits connected with music and sounds.'

'And?'

'Look at this.'

James had inserted bookmarks in the *Index*. He

127

turned to a page and pointed out an entry at the bottom of the page. 'Read for yourself.'

Sophie took the old book carefully on her lap. The print was small and she had to squint. 'Are you joking? It's in Latin, isn't it?'

'Go past that. Most of the entries are in Latin first, French second and then in English.'

'Ahh, I see it!'

If there be snaches of musik or plukking of strings or any kind of foreshortened bursting of musik ... then this may be an open cry for completion & relese of said spirit — and if in conjunction with chroma of illuminations and lanterns the correspondence will be so ... to wit, sapphire for a child or youth, green for a foundling, golden for a lost adulte & etc.

And if the snaches or plukkings can be identified in the greater piece then this may be an easy remedy for the calling soul and much relief given therein.

Sophie read the entry three times.
James fidgeted impatiently. 'Well?'
'It fits. Blue lights. Snatches of music.'
'It's the spirit of a child, isn't it?' said James.

'Trapped in that house.'

Sophie shivered. 'James, why do I suddenly feel very cold?'

'I do too. It's because up until now it's all been an adventure, a bit of a game. Now we're seeing what it's all about. And how real it is.'

Sophie looked up at a nearby gravestone marking the death of someone who died over a century ago. 'It's as real as that. And I'm scared.'

'We don't have to carry on, you know.'

'No, we don't have to. But we've been called, haven't we? All this. The dreams. The house. The *Index*. We've been chosen and I don't know why but for some reason because we can hear where other people can't hear. There is the spirit of a child or young person and it's trapped and in pain and it has called me and you to help it. I feel sick at the thought of going into that house again, but do you feel like you can ignore it?'

'No.'

'Exactly. No. But I wish we'd never started.'

James and Sophie sat hunched on the bench in the churchyard. They sat in a heavy silence, neither of them feeling they had any more to say about the matter; and as they sat, dusk gathered around their shoulders and alighted on the branches of the trees, and shadows settled on the angles of the stone tower and in the eyes of the gargoyles leaning from the church walls.

Because the house was such a large one, Mrs Royston felt sure there would be documents relating to it somewhere. She had promised to research into the history of the house, and she had been true to her word. She had a friend who worked in the Records Office of the local council, who had come up with a list of owners of the property before it was condemned for demolition.

The records showed that the house had been built for a gentleman farmer who owned much of the surrounding land at the time, and it was passed down through generations of the same family. So much for the records. But Mrs Royston's friend in the office had heard a story about the house.

As it passed down the line, one of the inheritors had a daughter, and it was said he doted on her. But in her early teens she became ill. The father spent all of his money on different doctors but none of them could find what was wrong. She sickened over a period of time and she died. The father, who was a good farmer, was heartbroken. He began to drink heavily and neglected his farm. The house was already starting to fall into disrepair when the land around it was sold off bit by bit.

'That is so sad,' said Sophie.

'What made her sick?' James said.

'As far as I know, they never did find out,' Mrs Royston said. 'The poor father was driven to distraction and he never recovered from the loss of his daughter.'

Sophie thought of the flash of music, and the hairs on the back of her neck prickled. 'The girl played the fiddle,' she said confidently. 'She played it for her father.'

'You can't possibly know that!' James said. He looked at Mrs Royston.

Mrs Royston shook her head. 'I can't say if Sophie can or can't know that. All you can do is trust your intuition, the pair of you. The extraordinary thing is that although you both experience it differently, you both feel – or hear – these things. If just one of you were reporting this to me, it could be seen as fanciful. Let's just say *something is up* and you don't have to convince me any further.'

'But what do we have to do about it?' Sophie pleaded.

'What does your intuition tell you about that?'

For some reason Sophie looked at the palms of her hands, as if the answer lay there. 'She's suffering. Her sadness and fear has chained a tiny scrap of her to the house. We have to help her.'

'We have to help her let go, don't we?' asked James.

Mrs Royston stared hard at him through the cloudy lenses of her dark glasses. James realised Mrs Royston was never going to direct them. She would help them, but they had to arrive at their own decisions.

'The *Index* says something about identifying the music. It says that spirits can be very attached to music for some reason.'

Mrs Royston said that lots of people connected music to places or to particular times in their lives. Lovers had special songs, for example. Music stirred deep memories in people, or brought to mind strong emotions. Music, she said, went much deeper than words. 'Whatever you decide to do, I'd prefer it if you don't go back into that house until we find a little bit more about what we're dealing with. All right? And now,' said Mrs Royston, 'who's ready for a cup of tea?'

132

12

'Should I be worried?'

Sophie looked up from her homework. Her dad stood in the doorway, gazing down at her. 'Should I be worried?' he repeated.

'About what, Dad?'

'Well, if you started to listen to a lot of death-metal music grinding out songs about suicide I might be anxious that you were going to do yourself in. If you'd joined a gun club and were scratching bent-nail tattoos into your arm I might be worried that you were unhappy. But every time I walk into your room I see lots of papers and information about local history.'

'It's interesting.'

'Right. So shouldn't a girl your age be listening to bleached bimbos going "Oooh-oooh baby you're so fine?" And reading low-IQ teen magazines, stuff like that.'

'Dad, give us a break.'

133

'It's just kind of *specialist* is all I'm saying.'

'It's to do with history homework,' Sophie lied casually. 'Background and all that.'

Her dad twitched his nose, not buying her story for one second. 'Pretty thorough research, I'd say.'

'Yup.'

He shuffled in the doorway. 'Where's Suki these days? You haven't had her round here for a while.'

'Dad! I'm trying to do my homework here!'

Sophie's dad finally left her to it. She closed the file she was looking at. She'd borrowed some archive material from the library and some photo-copies of Victorian newspapers, looking for information about Ravendale but finding none.

It was getting late, so she tidied her room, dumping the papers on her desk. She changed into her pyjamas, brushed her teeth and kissed her mum and dad goodnight. Then she got into bed and fell into a heavy sleep.

To be awakened at about three o'clock in the morning by the sound of fiddle music. The music was coming from outside the house, immediately outside the front door. Though Sophie knew that she was inside a shimmer because not only was the light a softly glowing crimson and gold, but because some of the musical notes were passing into the house, through the walls, not as sound exactly but as ribbons of colour in which musical notations of crochets and quavers comprised the ribbons.

But it was cold – unusually cold – so Sophie put on her dressing gown and made her way downstairs. The music had become more excited. It was a jig or a reel – she didn't know the difference between the two – and it was played at high speed. Sophie opened the door and there before her, floating a few inches from the ground, was a young woman – barely any older than herself, looking not at her but at the nimble fingers of her playing hand as she stroked the instrument to a frenzy. The bow in her right hand barely touched the strings of her fiddle and it glowed with the same eerie blue light Sophie had seen at Ravendale. The girl was dressed in a long grey skirt and soft brown leather boots. She wore a green scarf knotted at her pale throat. Her hair was long and dark and tied at the back, and she played the music in a kind of fiery trance. Though her eyes never met Sophie's, they were also made of the same blue light that illuminated her bow.

The music conjured up a terrible loneliness and a yearning for home. It carried inside itself the swell and fall of the waves and the taste of salt. It made Sophie want to cry. Then it picked up in speed and seemed to reach a breakneck pace until quite without warning the girl's fiddle shattered into tiny pieces and her bow whipped itself against the frame of the door, breaking itself into two parts. The girl herself was instantly carried up into the dark sky in a terrible rushing, until she became a tiny silver and shimmering dot in the heavens, like a fixed star.

Sophie looked down at her feet. Shattered fragments of the fiddle and bow had arranged themselves into a single word: *YOU*.

Sophie looked up at the stars again. She clasped her dressing gown at her throat, so cold it was. She could see her breath condensing on the air, thick and white. She closed the door and went upstairs. Even with all that noise, her parents seemed to be sleeping on.

She got back into bed and soon fell back to sleep.

'What are you doing here?' James held the door open just a crack, looking white-faced and quite horrified to see Sophie.

'I had to come and tell you something.'

'Tell me what?'

'Aren't you going to let me in?'

Sophie had woken early and scrambled out of bed. She prepared her school things quickly, polished off breakfast and muttered some rubbish to her mum about going early to school for a rehearsal for a school play.

'School play?' her mum had said, still somewhat sleepy and taken aback to see Sophie speeding around the house like a bolt of white lightning.

'Love you! See you later!'

She'd hastened to the address James had given her. It wasn't difficult to find. The house had a neglected air and the door behind which James now seemed to be cringing could badly do with a coat of paint, though Sophie was too excited to take account of any of that.

'Let you in?' James looked over his shoulder as if someone in the house lurked behind him. 'Why would you want to come in?'

'Because, you drip, I've got something to *tell* you!'

'Uh? Can't you tell me from there?'

'What???'

'Can't you just . . .?'

'James! I practically ran here to tell you something. Open the sodding door and let me in, will you?'

'I can't let you in,' he wailed.

'Why ever not?'

'My dad. He's ill.'

'So, is he sleeping? I'll be quiet. If he's awake you can introduce me.'

'Sophie, you have to go away.'

'You're joking!'

'No, I'm not. Tell you what, wait there for ten minutes and I'll get ready for school and we'll walk together.'

To Sophie's utter astonishment, James closed the door on her. She didn't move a muscle for a few moments, then retreated down the path. Then she stopped. *No*, she thought, *I'm not having this*. She returned to the door. She could see that James was still there, lurking behind the frosted glass.

Sophie crouched down and opened the letter box. Putting her mouth to the letter box she said, 'You let me in or I'll never speak to you again, James. I absolutely mean it.'

She stood up and waited. After a few moments the door opened fully and an unhappy-looking James stepped back to let her in. As soon as she was inside, Sophie sensed something was amiss.

It wasn't so much that the house was untidy or dirty (though in truth it was both, a bit). It was more that everything was in the wrong place. Sophie could see a pile of towels on the stairs, as if someone planned to take them upstairs and then had forgotten and had put a number of books on top of them. Pairs of shoes were on the telephone table by the door and the telephone itself had slipped down the side of the table. And even from where she stood she could see that an armchair had been set up in the kitchen in front of a television set.

Sophie looked at James, who was still holding the door ajar. He wouldn't meet her gaze. Instead he gently closed the door. 'Where's your dad?' she asked him.

'Upstairs. Asleep.'

He brushed his finger under his nose and she knew he was lying.

'There's no one up there, is there?'

'Shhh! You'll wake him.'

Sophie ignored him and immediately began walking up the stairs. She got halfway before he called her back.

'Okay. Okay.'

She turned and came back down. 'Tell me the truth. You're living here on your own, aren't you?'

He nodded.

'James! How long has this been going on?'

James walked back through to the kitchen and slumped into the armchair. In the kitchen she could see that James had a camp bed made up by the back door.

Slowly it all came out. James's father had cleared off over a year ago. He left James a small bank account. There was barely enough in it to pay, by internet standing order, the household bills. James had retreated to the kitchen to reduce heating bills. He had an 'unofficial' Saturday job unpacking boxes at a local shop, and the money he earned from that was enough to feed himself. He knew that if he did his shopping late in the evenings the supermarket would sell off all the food going out of date, and he'd become expert at knowing when to go there and what to look for. There was no money to spare. He cooked for himself, did his own laundry and looked after himself when he was unwell.

No one at school or in any position of authority knew that as a fourteen-year-old boy he was living alone. On parents' evenings at school he forged letters from his father saying he was too ill to attend but was glad to hear that his son was doing reasonably well. They passed for the real thing and no one asked any questions. After all, he said, he only had to get through another two years and it wouldn't make any difference whether he was living alone or not.

Sophie was astonished. 'But you've got no one to care for you!'

James just snorted. He said his dad hadn't much cared for him even when he was there; that he'd spent all his time on the internet trying and failing to make money from selling and buying stocks and shares. It was a kind of obsession. Everything with his father was about appearances. Having the right car. Going to the right school. Wearing the right labels on your clothes. Having the right sort of son.

They talked about whether what James was doing was against any law. They decided it wasn't: that it was what his father had done in dumping him that was illegal. If he were to be found out James wouldn't actually be in any trouble but the local authorities would have to take him into care and he would be put in a special home or fostered out to a family or whatever it was they did. It all sounded horrific, and far worse than keeping up the pretence that everything at home was reasonable.

But it wasn't so much the practicalities or the legality of the situation that occurred to Sophie. It was this: how dreadfully lonely for James.

There was only one other person who knew. Mrs Royston.

James had noticed the strange figure of Mrs Royston in the supermarket. Who couldn't? She went there the same times that he did, shopping for sell-off bargains. After several evenings of seeing her, one time she'd stood in the checkout queue behind him. Out of the blue she'd said, 'You live alone, don't you?'

James had gone stiff with fear.

'Oh, I've startled you. I'm sorry. I'm just a nosey old woman who should mind her own business. Don't you worry, I'm not about to tell anyone.'

James didn't say a word to her that evening. He went home fretting about whether the old woman might tell someone after all, and for a week he waited for a knock on the door. It never came. Though he did wonder about the old woman – whose name he didn't know at the time – and if she somehow had special powers. She looked like a witch; or at least a creature of the shadows, with those awful large sunglasses she wore even in the brilliantly lit supermarket. Finally he decided to ask the old woman how she had seen through him. He wanted to know so that he could disguise whatever it was that had given the game away.

He was practically shaking on the day he approached her. She was studying a package of mixed salad that had been plastered with a yellow sticker.

'How did you know?' he asked in a shaky voice.

She turned and peered at him through those dark glasses. James had a strange feeling he was being measured from top to bottom. 'Can you believe the original price of this? A few chunks of potato, a lettuce leaf and a bit of thinly sliced carrot. There are places in the world where that original asking price would feed a family for six months. Is it a fair world, do you think? Is it a world where we have any right to feel good about ourselves?'

'No,' James had answered.

'Two things. One is that I have a nose for waifs and strays. Always have had. Spot 'em a mile off.' She'd smiled at him, and the darkness in her seemed to disappear at once. 'Secondly, you only have to look in someone's basket to know that they are shopping for one.'

James had glanced in his own basket. Small tins. Single portions. Individual packages.

She seemed to read his mind. 'I wouldn't worry if I was you. Most people are too busy racing round filling their baskets to notice you. I'm an old busybody who finds people in a supermarket more interesting than what's on the shelves. I'm no harm to you.'

'What else do you see?'

She had looked at him hard and then made as if to speak – but whatever she was about to say, she changed her mind and said instead, 'I can see you're very short of money. I've seen you weighing your decisions very carefully. I tend to shop for these bargains because I think it's simple-minded to pay more than one has to. You shop for them because you have no other choice.'

'You're right.'

'I often am. Do you mind dogs?'

'Eh? Dogs. Don't mind them, no. Quite like them, though I've never had one.'

Mrs Royston took a pen out of her bag and scribbled an address. 'I can't get around as much as I used to and I need someone to walk my dogs. I'll pay the going rate. Now I can't stay here chatting all evening.'

With that she'd turned to the checkout. No goodbye, no 'nice meeting you', nothing.

And that was how he'd met Mrs Royston. He did some dog-walking for her and a few other small jobs and that helped to supplement his income. She'd been his one friend until Sophie had come along.

'She's kept my secret safe, Sophie,' said James seriously. 'Will you?'

'But my mum and dad would help you James. They wouldn't give you away.'

'No!'

'Okay, okay, I won't say anything.'

'Your folks would mean well but they'd end up telling someone, who would tell someone else, who would inform the social services. They would come and get me, it's as simple as that. And what for? I'm doing fine on my own.'

Sophie glanced around at the camp bed and the chaotic kitchen. There was a laptop computer and a printer plugged in at the kitchen table, still displaying his homework. A half-eaten bowl of cornflakes sat next to the computer, from the moment her arrival had interrupted him. She didn't agree that James was doing fine, but said nothing.

'Anyway,' said James, 'what was it you came here to tell me?'

'She came to me, James. In the night.'

'Who came?'

'The girl. Who else, you idiot?'

'Gimme a break, I'm still half asleep.'

'She came to me playing the fiddle. It was the tune I'd heard. More of it. It was wild.'

'Did she leave you a message?'

'Not exactly. But I know what she wants. She wants me to help her. She's desperate for help. I just know it.'

'And how are we going to help her?'

'I don't know that. I just know we have to go back inside that house.'

James winced. 'Don't much fancy that idea. Plus Mrs Royston said we'd better not.'

'Fine!' Sophie almost shouted. 'I'll go in alone. You wait outside! Helpfully.'

Sophie knew perfectly well that James would never let her go into the house alone. But she wanted to tell him that this was no time for cold feet, that they'd come too far on this strange journey to back out now. She wanted to tell him that she was prepared to see things through to the end whether he did or not.

'I'm not saying I wouldn't,' he snorted. 'I'm just saying that I'm not looking forward to it. You have to admit that the house is totally creepy.'

'But it's all been creepy, James. The shimmers are creepy. The dreams. The messengers and the messages. It's something to do with the way we are. You and me. The way we're put together. For good or bad we're able to see things other people can't.'

'You're saying that *we* are creepy. Great. Now I'm a geek *and* I'm creepy.'

'Yeh,' Sophie smiled. 'You're a creepy geek. I'm a creepy cow.'

'I don't think you're a cow,' James said.

'And I don't think you're a geek. But you know what my judo teacher – sorry, *our* judo teacher – taught me about that? William said use your opponent's force in all things. He said they used to call him squint-eye when he was a kid. At first it hurt but then he learned it was easier just to laugh at it. So he used to wink at them with his squinting eye.

146

He said that if an arrow passes through the target it just drops harmlessly. Maybe at school if they thought you didn't care they would stop calling you names.'

'Speaking of school,' said James, 'we need to get going. Look at the time.'

'Tomorrow night would be good,' said Sophie, gathering up her school bag. 'I can tell my folks I'm going to the youth club or something. Now I see that you don't have to tell anyone about anything.'

'It has its advantages,' James said. 'But you promise you won't say anything to anyone about how things are here?'

'I won't breathe a word,' said Sophie. 'Finish your breakfast and let's go.'

13

At the end of the school day Sophie made a point of looking for Suki, to walk home with her. She knew that Amy had a gym class and she thought it would be a good opportunity to mend fences with Suki. But she couldn't find her, and walked home alone.

Anyway, she had other things on her mind. She passed the playground and the church, and her stomach churned to walk past the derelict house. She could hardly bear to look at it. James and she had admitted to each other that the idea of returning to the house the next evening scared them. But saying it and feeling it were two very different things. And as she turned from the path towards the washbrook, she saw Suki sitting on one of the wash-stones.

The wash-stones were three ancient clay-coloured boulders worn smooth by the passage of water over hundreds of years. And for centuries it was said that local women came down to the brook to wash their clothes in the old way: to wet them, to rub them, and to slap them clean against the smooth stones. The stones had been pulled out of the brook and assembled in a ring as a monument to their history.

Suki sat on one of the stones, looking down at her hands and examining her fingernails. On one of the other stones sat a young man in a long dark coat. He was a strange and unpleasant-looking figure. His face was pale, and snake-like tattoos stood out brightly on the backs of both of his hands. He sat with his legs apart and his arms resting on his knees, just above the dangling straps of tall leather boots. He had his head ducked close to Suki's ear and he seemed to be whispering to her.

If this was Suki's boyfriend Sophie didn't think much to him. She thought perhaps she had better not interrupt them. They were playing at love-birds and Sophie didn't want to intrude. But she desperately wanted to put things right with her friend, so she decided to announce her presence.

'Suki!' she shouted.

In the same moment that Suki looked up, the young man let himself slide from the stone and onto the grass behind Suki. Sophie walked up to her friend with a ready smile, but the smile vanished when she realised the young man was gone.

'Hi,' Suki said gently. 'I've been waiting for you.'

'Where's he gone?'

'What?' Suki said. 'Who?'

'Come on, Suki, I saw him.'

'Saw who?'

'Oh, come off it, Suke! Don't play games!'

Suki just blinked. Sophie thought how tired she looked: drained and pale, with bags under her eyes as if she wasn't sleeping well.'

'Come on,' Sophie said, 'I won't tell anyone. Is he your fellah?'

Sophie could see why Suki would want to keep him a secret. He must have been at least ten years older than she was, and probably more. She thought maybe that he'd come from the children's playground, where drug-users sometimes congregated at night. There were some pretty unsavoury characters hanging around that place, even in the daytime, and occasionally they would leer or whistle at the school-girls as they filed past. If Suki had got mixed up with one of those druggies, there was no way she would want her friends or her family to know.

'What are you talking about? Sophie?'

'I'm talking about your boyfriend, wherever he's hiding.'

'Sophie, you're insane.'

'Come on, Suke, I've seen you with him two or three times now.'

Suki got off her seat. 'You know what? I avoided walking home with you from school tonight. Then I got here, where we used to sit together, and I felt bad, 'cos you've always been my best friend. So I decided to wait. But you're just so weird lately. Weird, Sophie, weird. Ever since you've been parading round with geek-boy.'

'But I saw you!' Sophie protested.

'Saw what? I'm sorry but I've had it with you and your weirdness, all right?' Suki folded her arms and walked away hurriedly, towards the footbridge.

'Suki!'

'Can't be arsed!' Suki shouted without looking back. 'Forget it.'

Sophie was crestfallen. Her attempt to patch up her friendship had just made things worse, and she didn't even know why. She looked at the wash-stone where the young man had been sitting. It glistened with an oily, snail-like mucus running from it. Suki's seat was perfectly dry.

Sophie reached out and touched the slimy mucus on the other stone. It was slippery between her fingers. She brought it to her nose to sniff it. The smell made her want to throw up.

At supper time Sophie could barely eat. When her mum asked her what was wrong she said she felt a little sick, which was certainly true. There was a bad smell on her fingers that wouldn't seem to go away, no matter how hard she scrubbed them. But more than that, it was the prospect of going back into the house

She failed to get any school homework done, because she couldn't possibly concentrate. She spilled her drink before bedtime. She banged her elbow on the bedroom door-handle. She made her gums bleed when brushing her teeth. Yet she knew she had to go. She felt the fiddler girl had called to her and James, needing their help, and that no one else was around to finish the job they had started. Who could see a suffering child and not do anything about it? What sort of a person would walk away? Even though it terrified her, she knew that she would have to go back into the house. Even though Mrs Royston had advised against it. Of course it did occur to her that the simple act of returning to the house might achieve nothing at all. But she knew they had to try.

She desperately wanted to tell her mum and dad what she was doing, but it wasn't possible. They would try to stop her. Even though they themselves were not the kind of people to turn their backs on someone who was in trouble, they wouldn't let her go. Or even if they believed her and understood what she was doing for a single minute, then they would want to go with her, and somehow Sophie knew that would change everything and make the task impossible.

In the same way that she was able to glimpse spirits, and become aware of ghosts, and receive scraps of messages, she knew that you couldn't point them out to other people. It was something that only a *savant* could see or hear. Before you could even try to draw anyone's attention to the thing, it would already have gone. It would be like trying to roll up a shadow for them so that they could feel its texture, or like trying to catch light in a net. These things, Sophie knew, lived in a world at a tangent to our own. And for reasons she didn't understand their world occasionally overlapped our world, for about as long as a soap bubble on the wind before it popped and was gone. You either saw it or you didn't, and very few people did.

No, it was her duty to help, along with James, because only the two of them knew what was going on at the house.

Sophie tried to fall asleep. She kept hearing snatches from the girl's wild fiddle-playing. It was like some spirit was out to torment her. But this time she knew it was no spirit, no demon, no ghost:

this time the music was coming from her own mind and the terror she felt at the prospect of going back to the house.

Sophie covered her ears with her hands. But still the music went on, relentless, rising and falling, sometimes muted and sometimes like the screeching of birds. She couldn't shut it out. But with this wild music in her ears, she did eventually fall into a fretful sleep.

Only to be woken in the middle of the night by the sound of a distant knocking. She woke up in a gleaming light that was silver but streaked with fine red veins, as if she were suspended inside the albumen of an egg. She knew that she was inside a shimmer. She knew that she wasn't properly awake, but she knew this was not a dream either.

The knocking was coming from downstairs. She got out of bed and looked in at her parents' bedroom. They were sleeping on, undisturbed. The luminous display of the bedside clock shone back at her: 3:33. The knocking from downstairs became more insistent.

Sophie stepped carefully downstairs. The knocking was coming from the front door. The silver light around her was unsteady, like heat rising from a road on a baking hot summer's day. Her movement down the staircase disturbed it, sent it wobbling around her. Sophie was fearful that the light might pop, that the shimmer would break and that she would find herself back in bed.

At last she reached the door, drew back the security bolt and opened it to the night.

It was the hawker. The night hawker, the very first one she'd seen. Just as before he was exceptionally tall and wore a long grey coat, and once again the moonlight gleamed brilliantly on his silver buttons. But this time he stood at an impossible angle, at about forty-five degrees, and his feet weren't touching the floor. This time on his tray was a set of three Russian dolls of different size, the kind that fit inside each other. On the two larger dolls a jolly smile was painted, but the smallest of the three dolls had a hideous and ugly grin painted in angry black lines. The hawker's tray was held at the same crazy angle, and the dolls should have slid off the tray to crash on the ground, but they did not.

But more disturbing than all of this were the hawker's eyes. There was no white in them. They were small lakes of black oil, and in those dark pools Sophie could see herself reflected. Sophie felt a lash of pure terror and had to clamp her teeth together as the hawker's feet rose higher and his head moved downwards until he was floating in a horizontal position. Then, slowly, he began to spin. His head narrowly avoided the ground as he turned, and the spinning increased in speed. As he began to spin faster and faster a wind got up from somewhere behind him, playing havoc with the leaves of the nearby trees. The spinning became impossibly fast, until all Sophie could see was a black-and-white spiral, while the wind became a full-strength storm, thrashing at the branches. The spinning wheel diminished in size until it completely vanished, and the storm stopped abruptly.

Sophie's heart was grinding in her ribcage. She'd been holding her breath. She walked down the path and looked up and down the street for any sign of the hawker. There was nothing. The orange sodium streetlamps cast a dull glow up and down the empty street.

'This is not a dream,' Sophie said to herself.

She went back inside, closed the door and shot home the security bolt. Then she went back to bed. The music, at least, had stopped.

'Bad night,' said James when he joined Sophie to walk to school the next morning.

'Me too. I feel like I'm gonna throw, James, honestly.'

'The hawker?'

'Yes. He came. I've no idea what he was trying to tell me though. He came to you?'

'Yes.'

'Russian dolls?'

'Yes.' James looked grave. He had his head down and he was walking very fast. Every five or six yards Sophie had to put in a skip to keep up with him. 'We've just got to get through the school day. Then when it's dark we go in, do what we can then get out. Then it's over. If it doesn't work, that's it.'

'Right.'

'I mean, we'll have done our best.'

'Right.'

'What more can we be expected to do?'

'Slow down, will you, James! Any faster and we'll be trotting to school. And stop trying to convince yourself. We'll do what we can, that's all. Heck, please change the subject. I don't even want to think about it.'

But the fact was they had to walk past the house.

The school day dragged, and yet at the same time it went too quickly. Sophie, sick with anxiety about what might happen that evening, looked up from her work in history at Abby South and wondered if

James was suffering in the same way. James, at Castle, looked up from his maths lesson at about the same time and questioned whether Sophie was as nervous about the operation as he was. His heart was thudding in his chest, and it was still before lunchtime.

In the afternoon, James was rebuked for staring out of the window during English. At about the same time, a quarter of a mile away, Sophie was spoken to sharply for not paying attention during RE. The clock was ticking. Neither of them wanted the evening to come; and yet they both wanted the day to be over.

When the bell at Sophie's school went at the end of the day, the sound pierced her like a sword to the heart. There was no bell at James's school. But at the end of the last lesson, it was as if he heard one: not like the bell at Sophie's school, which was electronic and shrill, but like a gigantic brass bell tolling in some doomy temple far, far away.

Sophie had to sit down in the cloakroom. She felt dizzy. James went into one of the cubicles in the boys' toilets, where he promptly threw up.

They walked home together in silence. They both knew that they could simply tell the other that they wanted to back out. After all, there was nobody making them go back into the house. No one was standing over them with a gun. And if they'd wanted to, they could easily persuade each other that it had all been in their imaginations. They could just laugh it off, and try to forget about the whole thing.

But there was no backing out. And each knew what the other would say if they even brought up the subject. It was real, all of it. They were on a shining path that had started with the shimmers, and then there were the visits from the hawker, and the inspirational messages that followed. Then there had been the book, the *Index*. There was no doubt that it was all real, and that somehow it was all meant to be. Neither of them could leave the spirit girl to suffer in that house any more than they could drown a puppy in the canal.

There was no going back.

'Seven o'clock?' Sophie said before turning away for home.

'Seven o'clock,' James said grimly.

And at seven o' clock they met at the end of the street. Sophie hadn't liked lying to her parents about going to the youth club but she felt there was no alternative. Her dad had offered to come and collect her in the car when it finished, but she'd hurriedly told him that they would be walking back together as a group, and that he needn't bother.

Though she did leave a note in her bedroom, for anyone to see. It didn't say that she and James were going there. It simply read: *Ravendale, the old house by the church. Try there.* If anything went wrong, she hoped her parents would figure it out.

It was dark when James arrived. A breeze had blown in from the west and a fine rain had made the street slick and wet. The streetlamps had come on and the orange light reflected dully from the greasy road.

James arrived with a large torch sticking out from his coat pocket. Sophie too had the sense to bring a torch along with her. At least they would be able to see their way around the house. They turned and made their way towards the house. She flicked up the hood of her coat against the rain. James copied her.

'Did you find any more in the *Index*? Have you brought it with you?' asked Sophie.

'No need. There was nothing in it beyond what we already saw.'

The rain started to come down more heavily as they made their way to the house. When they got there absolutely no one was around. The nearby houses looked cosy enough, and both knew what the other was thinking.

'Well,' Sophie said, 'the sooner we get inside, the sooner we can get out and go home. Same way in as last time?'

14

Sophie and James scrambled inside the house in exactly the same way as they had got in before. The wood panel lifted easily from the window frame. James wondered if someone else had been in recently. With Sophie going in first they dropped lightly from the window ledge and onto the landing, almost without a sound. James switched on his torch, flashing it around the damp walls.

'Can you hear something?' said James. 'Like a vibration?'

Sophie could indeed hear a gentle buzzing and a tiny vibration that went through the house. It seemed to come from very far away. It was very faint. So faint that Sophie didn't know whether she could feel it rather than hear it. 'Like a cat purring?'

'Kind of.'

Slowly they descended the staircase. Suddenly James froze.

'What is it?'

'I heard something.'

They both strained their ears. There was nothing. 'Maybe it was rats,' said James.

Then they heard a snigger of laughter come from somewhere in the house. Sophie grabbed at James's arm. Her blood ran cold. 'I heard it that time.'

All went quiet. James and Sophie looked at each other, their eyes bulging in the dark, both not wanting to stay but neither ready to suggest that they quit. Then there was another snigger, followed by the tinkle of a girl's laugh. It seemed to echo around the house.

'She's here,' Sophie said. 'She's really here, isn't she?'

James nodded.

'I'm scared,' Sophie said.

James flashed his light around the walls again. The light only made the shadows jump. The shadows pressed in on them and the house seemed colder than ever.

'I don't think I can do it,' Sophie said. 'I don't think I can stay.'

They listened hard again. There was no further sound. Then there was a loud bump and three or four voices laughed, all together.

A female voice shrieked and a boy's voice was heard to shout something. This was followed by more laughter.

'That's no ghost,' James said. 'Someone else is already here.'

They listened hard. Four voices were raised in shouting and good-natured arguing. Then there was a long silence again.

'Come on,' whispered James. They soft-footed down the stairs, James shining the torch in front of him, Sophie hanging on to his sleeve and following behind. 'It's coming from that room at the back of the house.'

When they reached the downstairs hall they could see soft orange light filtering from the room where they'd found the mattress and the rubbish. Suddenly there was talking again, and giggling. Then sudden quiet again.

'I know that voice,' Sophie said.

James switched off his torch as they edged nearer the room. The orange light was coming from a number of lighted candles placed around the mattress. Seated on the mattress were Suki and Amy, along with a couple of boys whom Sophie didn't recognise. The long silences were explained by the fact that the two couples were locked in a snogging marathon.

They were embracing and kissing, long and hard, not seeming to need to come up for air. Amy was leaning her back against the wall and her partner had his hands either side of her face. Suki's knees were drawn up underneath her, and her kissing partner had a hand on each of her shoulders. All four of them had their eyes closed.

There was nothing in this scene that would have shocked or upset Sophie. What her friends were doing wasn't anything unusual for teenagers of their age. But still Sophie was horrified. And what horrified her was something else altogether.

Behind Suki as she enjoyed her kissing marathon with her boyfriend was a fifth person. It was the tattooed young man Sophie had seen in Suki's company before. The young man she'd spotted on the washbrook footbridge and later sitting with Suki on the wash-stones.

He seemed to be stroking Suki's long dark hair as she kissed her boyfriend. Stroking her hair yet not quite touching it, keeping his long white fingers the tiniest fraction of an inch away from her hair so that his fingers were close enough to cause the prickle of static electricity in Suki's hair without him actually making contact. This fifth person was utterly focused on Suki. He sat cross-legged behind her as he worked away, almost combing her hair with his pale hands.

He was sitting cross-legged but was floating,

suspended in air, perhaps twelve inches or more from the floor.

The soft orange light from the candle made his skin look almost green. His teeth, bared as he stroked the air a centimetre from Suki's head, looked yellow and unless she was mistaken they were filed to sharp points. His eyes were like the eyes of a cat and they were half-closed in pleasure at his game. And he was *purring*.

His purring set up a strange vibration around the room and all over the house. It was the source of the buzzing they'd heard earlier. It seemed to be coming from deep in his chest.

Sophie looked at the face of this creature and felt a wave of spiritual dirtiness come off him like an odour, like a foul puff of wind. The sight of him almost touching her friend turned her stomach.

'Do you see him?' Sophie whispered to James.

James nodded. His eyes were flared open at the sight.

'Floating?' She wanted to be sure her eyes weren't playing tricks.

He nodded again.

'Suki doesn't even seem to know that he's there,' she whispered. And then wished she hadn't. Because the vibration, the purring, suddenly stopped.

Still hovering a few inches above the ground the tattooed figure began to turn away from Suki and towards Sophie and James with incredible slowness. When he had turned one hundred and eighty degrees it was clear that his golden cat's eyes remained half-closed. His head was tilted to one side at a bad angle and his lank hair fell partially across his face. 'But I know,' he said, revealing his razor-pointed yellowing teeth and lips that seemed to be not pink as with all human beings, but the colour of the juice of blackberries. 'But I know that *you* are here.'

And with that a wind snuffed out all of the small candle lights, and both Amy and Suki were heard to scream.

15

When James flashed his torch, both he and Sophie could see something that Suki, Amy and the two boys couldn't. It was the evil tattooed figure. He stood with his hands cupped either side of his mouth. His cheeks were inflated like a giant puffer fish, baring his sharpened yellow teeth, and blowing at the already snuffed candles.

Amy, Suki and the boys blinked into the torch beam. 'Who's that?' said Amy.

'It's me, Sophie. Me and James,' said Sophie.

Amy and Suki screamed again, but this time with relief. Then they laughed. 'What the heck are you doing here?' said Suki.

'You scared us,' said Amy.

'Yeh,' said one of the boys sourly, 'don't do that.'

The other boy was already relighting the candles. Each time he lit one it was blown out again.

'What are you doing here?' Suki asked again.

'Come for a snog?' said Amy. 'I was right about you two!'

'I can't get these to light,' said the boy trying to ignite the candles.

Sophie and James both had their eyes on the demon, who was now crouching and still blowing out the candles every time they burst into flame. 'No,' said Sophie. 'You need to get out of here.'

'What?' said Suki. 'Why?'

'You don't want to know.'

'What are you on about?'

'Something bad is going to happen,' said James.

'Still got your weird friend, I see,' said Amy.

'Who is this freak?' said the first boy. 'He's creeping me out. What's he staring at?'

'I can't get these candles to light. They keep going out.'

'Sophie,' said Suki, 'if you want to join in the fun then do so. But you could stop being so bloody weird.'

'If you know what's good for you,' said James, 'I'd leave this place pretty quickly.'

'Who the hell is this freak?' the boy said again.

'Will someone else have a go with these candles?' said the other boy.

'There's someone else in this room,' said Sophie.

The four instantly froze.

'The reason you can't light the candles,' said James, 'is because he keeps blowing them out.'

'That's not funny,' said Amy.

'I feel cold,' said Suki.

'You two are a real pair of downers,' said the first boy. He was glancing all round the darkened room, not seeing anything in James's torch beam. But he had his own torch and he flashed it round the room.

'Know what?' said the boy who'd been struggling to light the candles. 'The party's over anyway. I'm out of here. You lot coming?'

'Good idea,' said Sophie.

He was already moving towards the door. Amy followed him with the other boy. 'Sophie, you just spoiled a really good evening,' she said nastily. 'I don't know what's wrong with you. Come on, Suki, let's go.'

Suki made to follow, but as soon as she took a step the tattooed beast crossed the floor and grabbed her hair. Suki's head was jerked back.

'I'm caught on something,' Suki said. 'My hair is trapped.'

They heard Amy and the boys scrambling up the stairs and out of the window. Amy's voice was heard calling Suki, but they were already outside.

Now James had his torch shining in the demon's face. He and Sophie could see clearly what Suki couldn't. 'Let her go,' said Sophie. 'Just let her go.'

The tattooed beast turned his eyes on Sophie. In a soft whisper he said, 'She's mine.'

'No,' said Sophie. 'We're here to stop you.'

'My hair is all caught up!' Suki said, a note of panic coming into her voice. 'Who are you talking to?'

'Don't interfere,' said the demon.

'I don't know,' said Sophie. 'But for some reason I don't understand, he's afraid of me.'

'You are out of your depth,' whispered the beast.

'Help me!' shouted Suki. 'What's happening, Sophie? What's happening?'

The tattooed creature blinked. His eyelids were like those of a reptile. He held a hank of Suki's hair. Every time Suki tried to crawl forward he yanked back her hair, though she had no idea of what was holding her or whom her friend Sophie was talking to.

'Let her go,' Sophie said once again, very calmly.

The beast pulled Suki's face closer to his. 'This one? You want me to let this one go?' Then he reached out his long tongue and licked Suki's face.

Suki screamed. Though she couldn't see or hear what was holding her by the hair, she could feel the beast's vile wet tongue on her face.

'Let her go,' Sophie repeated.

171

'Why? Why would I do that?'

'Let her go and take me in her place.'

'Don't do that,' James said quickly.

'It's all right,' said Sophie. 'It's all right.'

'Trade her?' said the demon. 'Trade her for you?'

'Yes.'

'I don't like it,' said James.

'With your agreement,' said the demon, suddenly releasing Suki's hair, 'it's done.'

The demon disappeared, and in that same moment all of the candle flames were re-ignited. James and Sophie were left darting glances at every corner of the room, looking for their enemy. But he was gone, utterly.

Suki ran her hands through her own hair. 'What just happened?' she wailed. 'What's going on?'

'I can't explain,' Sophie said. 'But we should get out of here, now.'

They left the candles to burn. Sophie pushed Suki ahead of her and James came up behind, still looking over his shoulder. They climbed the stairs onto the landing and one by one they got onto the windowsill and dropped down.

Amy and the two boys were still there, waiting for Suki.

'What kept you?' Amy said to Suki.

Suki didn't answer.

'Thanks,' one of the boys said to Sophie and James, 'for wrecking a great evening.'

'Yeh,' said the other. 'Remind me to invite you both next time.'

'You used to be good fun,' Amy almost shouted at Sophie. 'I don't know if it's just you or if it's because you hooked up with this loser but I've just about had it with you!'

James suddenly lost his temper. 'Have you any idea what Sophie just did for Suki? Any idea, you little shit? What she just did for all of you?'

'Did for all of us?' one of the boys snapped back. 'What the hell are you talking about?'

Sophie was about to speak but Suki interrupted. 'Leave it,' she said.

'What happened in there?' Amy wanted to know.

'Just leave it,' said Suki. 'All of you. I just want to go home. Sophie, I'll see you tomorrow.'

With that she turned and walked away from the house, back in the direction of the washbrook bridge. Amy and the boys were still glowering at James. But first Amy and then the boys turned to follow Suki home.

James and Sophie watched them all go until they were silhouettes on the footbridge. 'Are you okay?' said James.

'I think so.'

'Do *you* know what you did?'

'No. It just seemed right at the time.'

'I still don't like it. I don't know what it means.'

'No,' said Sophie, 'I don't like it either.'

'Come on,' James said. 'I'll walk you home.'

16

Sophie slept badly. She had nightmares. Not shimmers; just plain ordinary terrifying nightmares. Not dreams of the tattooed demon and his lascivious, licking tongue, but dreams of being lost, or of drowning, or of being unable to get home. In one dream she found that everyone spoke in a language only she couldn't understand. All these nightmares passed in a single night.

She knew that she had made a trade. But at what cost, she had no idea. That deal had been struck as surely as if gold and silver coins had passed between her and the tattooed beast. What she had no way of knowing was the value she had placed on herself when she had struck that trade.

'You okay, darlin'?' Sophie's mum said at breakfast the next day. 'You look pale.'

'I'm fine.'

Her mum placed the palm of her hand on Sophie's brow. 'And you look tired.'

'Didn't sleep too well last night, that's all.'

'Hmm. Maybe a few early nights is what you need.'

'Maybe. Anyway, I'd better get off to school.'

Sophie saw her mother look at her strangely before she left for school. It was a wet morning. The road was rain-slicked and oily. Cars slewed by, their tyres hissing on the road. The sky overhead was the same oily-grey colour as the road.

She met up with James. 'Okay?' he asked.

'Okay. But bad night.'

James nodded. It was all she needed to say for him to understand. They walked on in silence. When they got to the washbrook, Suki wasn't there waiting for them, as she usually was. They waited five minutes. 'She's not coming with us,' Sophie announced, and they moved on.

Sophie saw very little of Suki that day. Suki was avoiding her, that was clear. Amy was pleasant enough, but brisk. They were distancing themselves from her.

In some ways Sophie was relieved. It meant that she wouldn't have to discuss what had happened; that she wouldn't have to try to explain things that she couldn't begin to explain. But it also meant that she felt lonely and adrift.

She walked home from school alone that

evening, because James was staying behind for swimming practice. She had to pass by the church and the children's playground, but she couldn't bring herself to walk past Ravendale House. Instead she took the long way round, but before she did she stood on the washbrook footbridge and looked back at the house, whereupon a strange thing happened.

There was a bird perched on the chimney of the house. A bird she couldn't name. Perhaps it was a kestrel or something only slightly smaller. It perched on the chimney and appeared to be looking at her. Sophie thought little of it until it suddenly swooped, wings at full stretch, directly towards her.

Sophie was hypnotised by the flight of the bird. She could see its brown speckled wings and its sharp yellow beak as it swooped down. She waited for it to pull out of its dive and fly over her head. But it didn't. It flew right at her, and struck her exactly at the point below her ribcage.

Sophie felt the impact like a tiny fist hitting her. Though it didn't hurt, Sophie felt a shock of heat passing through her. She saw clearly that the bird passed into her and there was a bang of blue light in her brain. Her skin flushed hot and cold and goosebumps rippled wildly across her skin. Sophie doubled up, not in pain, but in perplexity.

When she straightened up again, holding her hand at the point where the bird had passed into her, she looked around her. She was searching for the bird. Although she knew that the creature had flown inside her, she also knew that this couldn't be. It was impossible. The bird must have collided with her and bounced off. It had to be on the ground somewhere, wounded perhaps, flapping with a broken wing.

But there was no bird to be seen. Sophie collected her breath. She looked back at the house once more, before she hurried home.

'Very strange.' These were Mrs Royston's only words on the subject of the bird as reported to her by Sophie. She sipped at the tea Sophie had made for her and munched thoughtfully on a ginger biscuit. 'Very strange indeed.'

'Did you find anything about the spirit we told you about?' James asked. They had told her all about the spirit Sophie had seen haunting Suki, but they kept quiet about the fact that they had gone into the house against Mrs Royston's advice. They thought the old lady would be cross with them.

Mrs Royston had been busy researching the *Index*.

'Perhaps. Bring the *Index* over here. Lay it out on

the table and I'll show you what I've found.'

Mrs Royston had marked the pages with strips of purple silk. She turned to a page and pointed to a paragraph with her little finger. A paragraph in Latin was followed by one in French, and underneath in smaller print, some notes in that curious English of the *Index*.

> There be a harmful *mazzikim* who may be a species of *Incubus*, some call a Gozard. Here be a nasty infestation of the lower rank of the third shelf of daimon. His smell offends. He will seek out a young girl or virgin and draw energy and life's cheer until she has none and but woe & she may linger a death. His favourite trick is to light upon a one that her friend with *clearvision* may intervene in her place. He is drawn to *musik* and drawn out by *musik*. You shall know him by his smell and because on his arms he bears the marks of the *mazzikim*. The Gozard is easily despatched by a forthright manner and angry words.

'Can you make sense of any of that?' James asked.

'Some of it,' said Mrs Royston. 'Everything in italics is cross-referenced to another entry in the book. I stumbled across this when I followed the *musik* references. The *clearvision* refers to anyone with the capacity to see the spirit and demon world. That means you two, who have the clearvision.'

'What is a mazzikim?' asked Sophie quietly.

'It's a name for one of the harmful types. The *Index* lists friendly and unfriendly spirits altogether.'

This thing was waiting for me, thought Sophie. *He lured us to the house. Then he lured me into making the trade. He wasn't really after Suki, he was after me. That was part of his game.*

'He is the one who made that girl sick, isn't he?' blurted Sophie. 'When she lived in the house in the old days. She played music and I'll bet she had the clearvision, too. He sucked the life out of her, and those doctors could do nothing for her. Does it say anything about dealing with a Gozard in the *Index*, Mrs Royston?'

'Well, as far as I can make out it just tells you to swear at the thing. You know: use bad language on it. I've heard that before, actually. Anyway, don't panic. If it was going to attack you immediately it would have done so by now.'

'No, it's not his way, is it? He prefers the long-drawn-out suffering.'

'Look, don't jump to conclusions,' said Mrs Royston. 'We don't know that any of this is true.'

Mrs Royston still had her head in the *Index*, talking about other references in the book that might or might not have something to do with it. With Mrs Royston occupied, James touched Sophie on the shoulder. 'I'll fight him with you,' he whispered. 'You're not on your own.'

Sophie looked away. She looked at Sasha, Mrs Finny and Tara. All three dogs lay by the fire with their heads between their paws, and all three were watching Sophie.

17

For the next few days Sophie went to school, and she came home from school. All the time she was expecting something to happen, but there was no sign of the creature she'd encountered in the house. Her sleep was disturbed, and the worry put her off her food. Her mum noticed that she wasn't eating properly; her dad remarked that she looked pale.

Sophie found herself spending time alone, trying to work out what to do. She didn't even want James's company at these times. She found herself sitting on the bench behind the church, surrounded by the gravestones and hidden from the world by the surrounding trees.

Her eyes fell upon one particular gravestone. It was a tall grey slate stone, with copperplate inscriptions chiselled into the stone. It was one she'd looked at many times when she'd sat in this spot with James.

Lydia Liquorice, died 1872. Gone Before.

She looked again. *Born 1858. You were the same age as me*, thought Sophie. There was lots more writing on the stone – almost too much, ordered by the family who had lost her at such a young age. But behind all the scrolls and great loops and curls were two clear designs, lightly etched into the slate behind all the words. One design was of a fiddle and bow, and the other was of a bird.

Then Sophie realised. She stumbled over to the gravestone and on her knees she traced the outline of the bird. 'It's you, isn't it? You're the girl! You lived in that house! He drained the life out of you, didn't he? And this is your name. Lydia.'

Sophie almost wanted to put her arms around the gravestone and embrace it, but she stopped herself. 'I've been looking at you all this time, haven't I? Right under my nose!'

And it made her cry.

Judo class came round and even her sensei William remarked that Sophie was looking off-colour. During a break James told her that William had asked if she was okay.

'What did you say?' Sophie replied.

'I said you were okay.'

'Good.'

'You are okay, aren't you?'

Sophie didn't get time to answer. William called everyone and told the group they were going to focus on *Kuzushi*. 'Not just unbalancing an opponent,' said William, 'but destroying his stability. Okay, pair up.'

Sophie was going to work with James, but William made them change partners. 'No, Sophie, I want you to work with someone bigger and heavier than you.'

He teamed her with a seventeen-year-old boy called Ollie, a cheerful and gangly blond-haired lad who blushed easily but who was already a brown belt. On instruction from William they and the other pairs moved together. Sophie was thrown over easily.

'Do that again,' said William, 'while I watch.'

They took up position. Ollie stepped in towards Sophie and she grabbed his sleeve and collar.

'Relax!' shouted William. But in three seconds he had thrown her again.

'Try again, but relax,' said William.

They engaged again. 'Relax!' shouted William. But within a few seconds Sophie was on her back for the third time.

'You're trying too hard. Look, your teeth are gritted. We'll do it again until you learn to relax. Engage.'

But it was no good. Ollie was able to throw Sophie with ease. William made them engage again and again, until the point where Sophie thought William was just being mean to her. Sophie was thrown onto the mat nine times.

'Have a drink of water, Ollie,' said William. 'Sophie, come here.'

William took Sophie to the corner of the mat and made her sit down. 'This is something I learned from my Japanese sensei,' he said. 'You know what bamboo is?'

'Yes,' said Sophie suspiciously.

'You are the bamboo. Ollie is the wind. You know what bamboo does in the wind?'

'Bends?'

William nodded. 'Sometimes a ferocious wind can dig an oak tree out of the ground, where a bamboo will only bend. When Ollie comes and I shout *relax*, I want you to go soft. Bend with his attack. Then strike.'

William called Ollie back. 'Engage!'

Ollie stepped forward and grabbed Sophie's suit. 'Relax!' shouted William. But two seconds later Sophie was on the floor once more. 'Again!' shouted William.

Sophie was close to tears. She felt humiliated, to be thrown to the floor over and over; she felt embarrassed to be singled out for William's tuition without making any progress; and she felt weak and scared about everything else that was happening in her life.

'I said again!' William shouted.

Sophie sniffed and took up position. Ollie stepped forward and Sophie stepped in to grapple with him. As if from a great distance she heard William shout, 'Relax!' And she had an almost comical impression of Ollie rushing at her like a wind. Instead of stepping forward to meet him with all her strength, she let her body go limp. The lack of resistance made Ollie take a step forward and in that moment Sophie swept her hips across him and threw the much older boy onto the mat.

'Yes!' shouted Sophie. 'Yes!'

'Big learning day!' said William, smiling back at her.

Sophie skipped across the mat and hugged William.

'Normally it's enough to bow to your teacher instead of hugging him,' he said.

'Sorry, sensei.'

'It's okay.'

Ollie was on his feet. He was red in the face and rubbing his shoulder. 'Hey, I want to get my own back!'

'Not a chance,' said William. 'Unless you want to try it on me.'

'It was a relief,' James said when they were walking home from judo, 'to see you crack a smile in there.'

They were heading back to Sophie's house. James was going to fix up Sophie's webcam on her computer. He had found software on the net they could use to talk to each other for free.

'I know. But I suddenly got what William meant, after all this time.'

'You never answered me, you know. When I asked you if you're okay.'

'I don't know. I feel sort of tired all the time.'

'As if something is stealing your energy?'

'Yes, but there's been no sign of that awful creature.'

'The Gozard?'

'Yeh. Since it disappeared in the house it's like it has gone altogether. I'd love to ask Suki, but there's no point since she didn't see it in the first place. Though when I have seen her, I thought she was looking much better. Like the colour had come back to her face, and the sparkle in her eyes. Know what I mean?'

James nodded. He knew exactly what Sophie meant. It was a sparkle that had now vanished from

Sophie's eyes and a colour that had gone from her cheeks. She didn't look well any more, but he didn't like to say anything.

They reached Sophie's house.

'I think I'm just not sleeping well. All this stuff has made me scared and I keep popping awake at night expecting to find that vile creature sitting on my bed. Or something. By the way, Mum said you should stay for supper after you've fixed the webcam.'

'You haven't said anything about my situation, have you?'

'Not a word. Fix the cam and then come and eat something with us.'

It didn't take James long to download software from the internet and set up Sophie's webcam. 'I'll test it from my place later,' he said.

Over dinner James fielded lots of questions about his parents. Sophie noticed that his technique was to say little and offer very few details that he might be quizzed on. And then he would turn the question back on the person asking.

'What's your dad do for a living?'

'He's a stress analyst.' This was true, at least before he'd cleared off.

'What the heck's that?'

'Testing things like metal or plastic under stress.

But you're a water-listener! That's so cool. What does it involve?'

That was Sophie's dad dealt with, and when Sophie's mum asked James about his mother he simply said, 'She died.' This was also true, and was followed by a question about whether he had enough sauce on his pasta.

But while he was cleverly dodging all the leading questions, James was also noticing that while he was scoffing heartily – since a proper meal made a change from cheese sandwiches – Sophie hardly ate at all. She prodded her pasta around her plate but didn't often lift it to her mouth. He began to have a bad feeling about what was happening to his friend.

About an hour later James was back at his house and cranking up his computer to see if his new webcam connection with Sophie was successful. They had decided that it was a great way to keep in touch. His broadband bills were being met by his absent father, and beyond that there were no charges to pay.

He logged in, switched on his webcam and sent a test message to Sophie. Moments later her face filled the screen. They had a good visual connection, but although she could hear James, he couldn't hear her. James ran through a few things that she might do to switch on her microphone, and within a few minutes they had full communication.

'Loud and clear,' said James.

'Hey, this is good.'

'Don't forget to switch it off at night unless you want me to see you getting undressed for bed.'

'Creep!' said Sophie.

A tiny smile crossed Sophie's lips, and James felt a little sad. A few weeks ago that sort of remark would have had Sophie laughing, and she would have called him a lot worse than creep. It seemed to characterise how depleted she seemed lately. But at least they could be in contact whenever they wanted.

'Just one thing,' said James. 'You're too close to the camera. Can you move it back a bit? All I can see are your eyes and nose!'

'Like that?'

'More. Push it away from you. That's better . . . oh dear.'

'What's up?

'Don't move.'

'Why? What's wrong?'

'Sophie, is anyone in the room with you? Right now, I mean.'

'No. Why?'

'Just look around and check for me, will you?'

Sophie had a look round her room. 'No, no one here. Just me, that is. What's the problem?'

'I've got some bad news for you.'

'Oh yeh?'

'He's with you in the room.'

'Huh? Who is?'

And in answer to that, James only blinked.

Sophie froze.

Then she quickly scanned the room again. She saw nothing. 'Tell me you're teasing me. Please tell me that.'

'Wish I was, Sophie.'

'Where is he, exactly?'

'Standing at your right-hand shoulder.'

Sophie shivered. She waved at the air. She could neither see nor feel anything. 'Don't leave me, James. What's he doing?'

'Smirking. Looking right into the camera at me. Like he's pleased with himself.'

18

Sophie waited in the dark on the street corner. She shrank back under the shadows cast by the over-hanging branches of a cherry tree. It was late, after ten, and she was waiting for James. A chilly wind flushed the leaves of the tree and she shivered, even though she had a coat.

She'd pretended to her mum and dad that she'd gone to bed. She'd known what to do. Make a fuss of changing into pyjamas and saying goodnight; close bedroom door behind her, stuff a pillow in her bed, draw up the duvet so that it looked like a body sleeping underneath; change back into her clothes; slip outside while they watched the late-night news on television; close the door with soft click.

Easy. Too easy. Anyone could do it.

She wished it were not so easy. But she also knew what she had to do. Since James had reported to her that the Gozard was dogging her every move, and since it had made itself invisible to her, she knew she would go crazy if she didn't find a way to fight it.

Her teeth chattered. She told herself she was cold. But it wasn't the chilly night air that made her teeth chatter.

James arrived.

Again they had told Mrs Royston nothing about their plans, because they both knew she would advise against going into the house. But what she had told them was that they would know when they had to confront the Gozard. And she said that if they decided the time was right now, then right now was the time. They both agreed that they had to make their own decision about this and that the old woman, being unable to help them, would only hold them back. And things had come too far to simply do nothing.

'Did Mrs Royston find anything for me?' Sophie asked. James had agreed to ask her to go through the *Index* to see if there was any clue that might help Sophie – about how to make him reappear, about how to take him on, anything.

James shook his head. 'She said that she was out of her league, and that we know more than she does, and possibly even more than the *Index* tells us. She said trust yourself.'

'That's just great,' snapped Sophie.

'Well, I'm here,' James said fiercely. 'And at least I can see him.'

'I didn't mean to snap at you,' Sophie said. 'But tell me something. Is he here? Right now, I mean?'

'No. He's not here now.'

'Let's go and find him then.'

'Still sure you want to do this?'

Sophie shivered. 'I don't want to, no. But I don't have any choice. Do I?'

'No,' said James. 'You really don't have any choice.'

As they neared Ravendale a police patrol car cruised by them and the driver eyed them suspiciously. But there appeared to be some activity further away, under the streetlamp near the children's playground, where the drug dealers and their customers congregated at night, and the police weren't much interested in two fourteen-year-olds.

They waited until the patrol car had turned the corner before cutting across the grass and ducking behind the shadows of the house. By now they had no difficulty in getting inside. This was their third visit after dark.

As soon as they had dropped onto the landing they stopped still, listening. There was no sound. Not even the sound of woodworm gnawing the old beams of oak that barely held up the roof.

At least not for the first few moments. Then they heard it. Very softly, almost indistinct, but they both heard it together. That soft purring, as if from a cat.

'He's here,' said Sophie.

James swallowed hard. The sound of him swallowing seemed to fill the place. Then there was nothing but the soft purring.

Though they both had torches, there was a soft radiance coming from the same room in which they'd found Suki, Amy and their boyfriends. Sophie hoped against hope that they would find the four there again, but knew she wouldn't. The scruffy mattress lay in the corner as before, but this time the tea-lights and candle stubs had been arranged in a circle round the room and all the candles were burning softly.

'Empty,' said Sophie, almost with relief.

'Then you're not seeing,' James said, 'what I'm seeing.'

James could see him very clearly indeed. The Gozard was sitting right in the middle of the circle of tiny flames. Though sitting would be the wrong word to use: because the creature was floating, cross-legged, about a yard from the floor. He had his back to James, but he was smirking at both of them, because his head was on back to front.

James gasped. His hands trembled and his tongue

stuck to the roof of his mouth. He had to force his breath to come normally. Pure cold terror made a ringing in his ears.

Sophie remembered William saying in his judo lessons that it was vital to hold your head up, and that if you didn't feel strong then you should act strong. 'Show yourself,' Sophie said. She tried to sound commanding. She didn't know where this brave voice came from. It was a bravery she didn't feel.

There was a flicker in the room and after a moment Sophie was able to see exactly what James could see: the Gozard was levitating three feet above the ground in the middle of the burning candles. His body was turned away from her but because his head had rotated one hundred and eighty degrees, he was looking right at her. 'I decide,' he said. 'Not you.'

Sophie's heart felt like it was trying to punch its way out of her. She had to take deep breaths to control her breathing. 'Are all Gozards cowardly creatures?' she said.

At last the Gozard turned its body so that it aligned with its head. There was a look of surprise on its face. The smirk had retreated a little, but its rhythmic breathing continued to produce a soft purr. 'You know what I am.'

'We know,' said James.

'How? How do you know?'

Sophie put out a hand to James, so that he wouldn't answer. 'You killed that girl. The one who lived here.'

The Gozard blinked his heavy-lidded eyes like a reptile, and remained silent.

'She was beautiful and clever and she loved music. You drained her of life. Her name was Lydia.'

When Sophie mentioned the name of Lydia, the Gozard stiffened visibly and the purring stopped. The candle flames suddenly shrank to tiny points of light, almost snuffing themselves out. Then after a moment the Gozard relaxed again, the purring resumed and the candle flames returned to full strength. 'She was my pet,' he said.

'Your pet?' said James. 'You don't destroy your pet.'

'We all have to feed,' said the Gozard. 'How many animals did you eat this week? A chicken? A lamb? A calf?'

'Animals, not people,' said James, feeling bolder.

'From where I sit, it's all the same.'

'Well,' James said taking a step in front of Sophie, 'you're not going to be feeding from *her*.'

The Gozard turned his gaze on James. James felt a tickling in his brain, and he knew that the Gozard was probing him, somehow trying to read his mind. The tickling stopped. The Gozard shook his head slightly. 'What is a geek?' he said.

From out of the lining of his coat James pulled a heavy iron poker he'd stolen from Mrs Royston's fireplace. It made a brutal weapon. Almost sword-length, it was fashioned with a cruel barb at its end. 'Find out!' shouted James, and he launched himself into the circle of candle flame. With a shriek he brought the iron poker smashing down on the Gozard's head.

The Gozard's head cracked like eggshell and splintered into a thousand pieces. Each piece took to the air like a disturbed butterfly, fluttered there for a moment, and finally fell back into the place it had come from, reassembling the Gozard's face uninjured. The poker might just as well have passed straight through.

The Gozard merely blinked back at James.

In frustration James brought the poker down on the Gozard three more times, and each time the same thing happened to the creature's body or head. James was left furious and helpless, his eyes bulging and sweat bubbling on his brow. He'd done no damage at all to the Gozard.

'My turn,' said the creature.

19

The three black dogs watched Mrs Royston as she sat at the table making notes from the *Index*. Each dog sat upright with its front paws pushed in front, watching carefully for tiny signs. Sasha and Tara remained alert, ever watchful. Only Mrs Finny looked round when a coal shifted in the grate; then she put her chin on the rug in front of the fire, but like the other two dogs she fixed her eyes on Mrs Royston.

Sasha was the lead dog, and the other two took their cues from her. Sasha in turn took her cues from Mrs Royston, and Sasha was worried. One moment the house had been peaceful, with the dogs stretched out before the fire and Mrs Royston slowly turning the pages of the *Index*. Then Mrs Royston had said some small word, to herself, that had made Sasha look up.

The dog saw Mrs Royston put her hand to her chest. So well did Sasha know her mistress that that tiny gesture, along with the small sound she'd made moments earlier, was enough to alarm the dog and put her on alert.

Something was wrong. All Sasha could do now was wait for instruction.

Because Mrs Royston was an epileptic. And Sasha was one of those remarkable dogs that have been trained to warn their owners of an impending attack. No one quite knows what it is that the dog recognises. It's enough that it works. They sense a change, perhaps in the chemical balance of the epileptic's brain, perhaps something else. Three strong clear barks, followed by a pause, followed by three more strong clear barks is the trained response. It's enough to warn Mrs Royston – or any other sufferer of epilepsy lucky enough to have such a trained dog – to take their medication in order to fend off an attack.

In this case Mrs Royston was not about to have an epileptic seizure at all. Sasha knew that. But it was a side-product of the training that Sasha was super-sensitive to all of Mrs Royston's moods. Sasha was ever watchful. She knew when her mistress was happy, sad, angry, lonely, tearful, sleepy, distracted or worried.

In this instance what Sasha had sensed, in that moment when Mrs Royston had muttered a single word and placed her hand on her chest, was a cold wave of fear.

So Sasha watched and waited. And the alarm had transmitted noiselessly from the lead dog to the rest of her pack. Tara and Mrs Finny became alarmed along with her. And like their leader, they watched and they waited.

Mrs Royston squinted at the open book in front of her. She turned a page and referred back to another. 'This can't be right,' she said quietly. 'This can't be right.'

Sasha whimpered.

Mrs Royston looked up to see three pairs of dog eyes trained on her. She turned back to her book, took off her dark glasses and got her eye close up to the small print of the *Index*. Then she put her glasses back on and made another note. She leafed through several pages of the *Index*, looking for something she'd read earlier. She'd found a new reference to the Gozard.

'Half of the wretched thing is in Latin!' she said.

Sasha whimpered again.

'Why didn't I pay more attention in my Latin classes, Sasha?' She got up from her chair, grabbed her walking stick and made her way over to the bookcase. From the third shelf down she pulled a mighty, leather-bound dictionary of Latin. She had to tuck it under her arm to get it to the table. There she opened it up, and started to make a translation of something new she'd found in the *Index*.

'Well, Sasha, it does say *caveat*, and we all know that means a warning, like *beware*, but what's all this stuff? Hmm, Sasha? What's all this other stuff?'

Mrs Royston flicked through the dictionary making notes. Then at last she found a paragraph in curious English.

That the demon-hunter be not upended should know of this fine caveat, that there are spiritum of great malignant force etc. and whose guile is such that they may yet take on the apparel & all appearance of a lesser spiritum & or demon, thusly disguised as an easily overcome lesser form to wit a Gozard or some such weaker entity in order to wreak anger and vengeance. Thus the demon-hunter should adopt all martial powers etc and never and no while go unprepared into the fray with such a creature, for his evil be mighty. Take unto yourself this caveat not lightly.

What Mrs Royston learned from the *Index* was a very clear warning. There were demons, it said, dangerous demons, who often disguised themselves as some lesser and weaker entity, such as an easily dismissed Gozard. That was exactly the example it gave. In such a case, it stated, it was very important not to tackle these dangerous demons unprepared.

Quite suddenly, Mrs Royston lifted her head from the book and listened.

The three dogs quickened. Tara whimpered.

What Mrs Royston heard was a sound. It was like a high-pitched whistle. A single unbroken note.

'They're in danger, Tara.'

Tara barked once, loud and clear.

'I'm going to have to take a look. There's no other way. Oh dear, Tara, what have those children done?'

Mrs Royston took off her dark glasses and touched her fingertips to the temples either side of her head. The roaring started immediately. Even though her eyes were closed, a flickering of brilliantly coloured lights appeared at the corner of the blackness. Electric blue, acid yellow, citrus green and red like the tail-lights of cars at night, squirming like tiny snakes.

The lights gave way to snatches of pictures – pictures that flashed rapidly across her mind's eye, changing so fast that it was difficult to see what they all added up to. Sometimes the pictures opened out, like a fan; sometimes they shuffled like a pack of cards. But it all happened at a maddening high

203

speed. And always behind the rapidly changing images was a terrifying and ear-splitting roar.

Mrs Royston saw Sophie and James. They were holding hands, but they were flying. She clearly saw them flying through the night sky, the wind blowing back their hair. In the flashing images she saw the line of their flight from Sophie's house. She also saw where they were heading: Ravendale.

Other pictures began to make themselves clear. She saw a ring of lighted candles. In the middle of the candles she could make out the face of the demon – the Gozard – exactly as Sophie had described. The demon was laughing an ugly, jagged laugh, and as its mouth opened to laugh Mrs Royston could make out a pair of hands reaching from inside the mouth until a new head and body hauled itself out of the cave-like, laughing mouth. Then the image was replaced by a bird. Then, all over again, Mrs Royston saw Sophie and James hurtling through the night sky.

Mrs Royston fumbled for her dark glasses and put them on again. Instantly the roaring stopped and the dancing pictures vanished. It took a few moments for her to recover her breath, as if she'd been running. Mrs Royston turned and looked at her dog.

'That's right, Tara. I'm afraid those children have gone to the house. And that means they are now in grave danger.'

Mrs Royston struggled out of her chair, but as she did so an electric jolt of pain shot through her hip. She had to cling on to the side of the table to stop herself from fainting with the pain. Her arthritis was bad on damp nights like these and some evenings it was agony simply to get from one side of the house to the other. Like tonight.

Sasha barked once and ran to her side, licking at her hand. 'It's no good complaining, girl. I've got to stop those children going into that house, if they haven't got there already. Now where did that wretched boy leave his phone number?'

James had written down the number of his mobile phone on a scrap of paper. Mrs Royston had never called him on it. She disliked using the telephone at the best of times, and thought that carrying a mobile phone was a dreadful idea. But she had taken James's number in case of emergencies.

This was indeed such an emergency. James had called round earlier to talk to her about the *Index*. Now she realised what he was asking for. They hadn't said anything about what they planned to do that evening, but she saw clearly now that James had been trying to get information about how they might confront the Gozard. The Gozard which was not a Gozard.

She calculated that it would have taken James about twenty minutes to get to Sophie's place, longer if he was distracted on the way. She hoped that Sophie might have been late for some reason. She prayed that one of the million things which delay a teenage girl might apply in this case, if only to give a little more time. Then, she reasoned, they had to make their way to the house. There was still a chance that they hadn't yet gone inside. If only she could think where she had put the scrap of paper with the phone number.

As she moved across to the fireplace to look on the mantelpiece a fearful pain shot up her leg and across her hip. She winced and sucked in her breath. She sometimes put papers under one of the pair of brass candlesticks she kept on the mantelpiece. There she found various scraps of paper, supermarket coupons, her library card and other clutter, but no phone number. At last she remembered that she'd pinned it to the back of the cupboard door where she kept the dogs' leads, in case she needed to call him about walking the dogs.

It was a struggle just to get across the room, with arthritic pain shooting up her legs, but she managed to grab the note and shuffle to the telephone table. She dialled the number with trembling hands. The number rang.

A recorded voice came on the line. It wasn't James's voice. She tried again, and when she got the message service she realised that James wasn't going to answer. 'It's no good,' she said to the dogs. 'We're just going to have to go and stop them.'

Mrs Royston didn't drive. Whenever she needed to go shopping or anywhere else, she used a regular taxi firm. She dialled the number and ordered one immediately. Then she went to get her coat.

As she lifted her old sheepskin coat from the peg behind the back door another dreadful shooting pain crossed her hips, grinding her arthritic bones. She gasped out loud and stepped back, only to stumble against Sasha, who waited protectively behind her. Mrs Royston toppled backwards. The cupboard door was open and to steady herself she reached for the dogs' leads hanging behind the door. Her weight was enough to whip one of the leads off its hook, and she fell backwards, cracking her head against the skirting board.

As Mrs Royston lay on the floor, Sasha barked and licked her face. Tara and Mrs Finny prowled the room anxiously and every now and then Mrs Finny let out a distressed bark. It made no difference.

Mrs Royston lay unconscious.

20

The Gozard turned its reptile gaze on James. First James felt his fingers being loosened from his grip on the brass handle of the iron poker, simply by the power of the creature's gaze. It fell to the wooden floor with a clatter. Then he felt himself lifted off his feet and slammed against the wall. The damp old plaster on the wall shook and cracked at the impact. James felt all the air pass out of him. For a moment he thought he would pass out. He had to fight to get his breath back.

Instead of sliding down the wall he remained stuck to the plaster. He tried to shake himself free, to no avail. He could move his head and his legs but his back, his shoulders and his arms were glued to the wall. He was like an insect caught on flypaper.

'Let him go!' shouted Sophie.

'What is he to you?' said the Gozard. When he spoke, faint traces of smoke came from his mouth.

'Just let him go.'

The Gozard shrugged. Sophie saw something crawl out of its mouth. It was a cockroach. It crawled from its chin to its neck and disappeared inside its collar.

'Is he your boyfriend?' said the Gozard, and not in his own voice but in a girl's voice. Sophie recognised that it was her friend Suki's voice. 'Is he your boyfriend?' it said again, but this time in Amy's voice. It switched back to Suki's voice. 'Have you snogged him?' Then the Gozard cupped his hands to his mouth like a megaphone and it was Amy's voice again, shouting, 'Helloooooooooo! Anyone at home in Sophie's fat head?' Then back to Suki with, 'Not a *boy* by any chance, is it?'

While this was happening James was struggling to breathe. His lungs felt compressed inside his body. He almost fainted, and for a moment he seemed to lose consciousness altogether. And when he opened his eyes, he saw a shape in the wall across the room from him. It was a girl. She was dressed in Victorian clothes. Like James, her hands were splayed to the wall; but unlike him she seemed to be moulded from plaster and even brick where the plaster had dropped off the wall. She was embedded in the *wall*, like a white statue or like moulded plaster. Her eyes were closed. He knew she was long dead. He also knew that this was Lydia.

Lydia seemed to exist in a flickering white light. It was like the light of what Sophie called the shimmers, and it seemed to suffuse the rest of the room. James wanted to tell Sophie to look at her, to get her to turn her eyes towards the figure on the wall. He did his best to call out, but he could barely even croak Sophie's name.

And when he looked again, the image of Lydia buried in the wall had faded.

Meanwhile the Gozard kept repeating things in the voices of Sophie's friends, mocking things they might have said to her, until her ears were ringing.

'Let him go, you vile creature!' Sophie screamed at the Gozard. 'Let him go!'

The Gozard opened his mouth. More smoke came out. '*Let him go, you vile creature!*' he said, in an exact replication of Sophie's voice.

'I know what you are and I know what you've done,' Sophie said. 'You drained the life out of Lydia, the girl who lived here. You are a slow poison. Well, she called me here to help her, and that's what I'm going to do.'

'No,' said the Gozard, now in his own vile whispering voice. 'I called you here. I used her to call you. And you came.'

'I don't believe you. You wouldn't have given me the *Index*.'

'*Index*?' he said.

'I believe it was Lydia who brought it to this house. In the early days when you had just got your claws into her. She was desperate to get rid of you and she hoped the answer would be in this book. But she didn't know how to read it. Or how to use it.'

'Show me this *Index*.'

'I don't have it.'

The Gozard turned to look at James, still pinned to the wall. 'Does he have this *Index*?'

'No. It's safe. Where you can't get it.'

Pinned to the wall James heard all of this and could make no kind of response. He looked over again at where he saw the image of the girl embedded in the wall. She had come back. Just as before, her head had fallen to one side, and her eyes were closed as if for a long sleep.

And then in a shocking moment the girl opened her eyes, looking hard at James. Those eyes were red at the rim, and they seemed to pierce James like a sword. In that instant the candle flames shrank again, and James was released from the wall. He fell in a bruising clatter.

The Gozard reared back, as if attacked. Something had angered him. Suddenly he was outside the circle of flame, hissing like a cat, smoke leaking from his mouth, more cockroaches scuttling from between his teeth.

Sophie ran to James, helping to pick him up. 'What happened?' she whispered.

'It's Lydia,' said James. 'She's here somewhere.'

The candle flames leapt again, and at the same time the old mattress in the corner of the room burst into flames.

21

There was a hammering on the door. It got louder and at last it brought Mrs Royston round. Her dogs were barking and Mrs Finny was licking her face. She sat up against the wall. Her head was throbbing where she'd banged it.

The doorbell rang again and there was more hammering. A voice was calling her name. It was Hussein, one of her regular taxi drivers. 'Are you there, Mrs Royston? Can you hear me, Mrs Royston?'

'I'm coming,' Mrs Royston shouted. 'I'm coming. Stop banging on the door.'

The letter box opened and Hussein started to call through it to her. 'Was that you, Mrs Royston? Was that you? Oh praise to God! I was worried for you!'

Mrs Royston got the door open and Hussein burst in. He grabbed her by the shoulders. 'Really, are you okay?'

'Yes, yes, I'm fine.'

'I was so worried! I said please don't let anything

happen to my friend Mrs Royston! I said I will kill you God if you let anything happen to that woman! She's my best customer! If she's dying I lose thousands of pounds!'

'Let me go, you fool!' said Mrs Royston.

She knew Hussein was joking, and he in turn didn't mind her abuse. He was one of the kindest people she knew. Hussein often stopped his cab to call in and see if she wanted anything, or to just check on her. He'd been ferrying her to the supermarket and other places for over ten years. She had met his wife and his young daughter on several occasions. Any time now Hussein's wife was due to have their second child.

'Are you sure you are okay? You don't look too steady!' said Hussein.

'Come on. We're taking the dogs out.'

'What, at this time of the evening? It's dark, you old fool.'

'Never mind that, I'll explain in the car.'

Mrs Royston locked the door behind her and bundled the three black dogs into the back of Hussein's cab while she rode up front. It had been her plan to get Hussein to help her when she reached Ravendale. But she never had the opportunity to ask him, because Hussein had other things on his mind.

214

'Just after you called, I got another call to say my baby is coming, Mrs Royston! Can you believe how happy I am? So I'm going to the hospital right after I drop you, Mrs Royston. I said I have time to take Mrs Royston first! But can you imagine, Mrs Royston, when I get to your house and no one is answering the door! I said to God if you cause problems for Mrs Royston while I'm on my way to the hospital I will never speak to you again, God. Where are we going?'

And with Hussein chattering away happily about his forthcoming baby, Mrs Royston felt unable to ask for his help. When the cab pulled up outside Ravendale House, she got out and opened the door for the dogs to jump out, too. She clipped each of the dogs onto a lead. It wasn't until that moment that Hussein looked anxious. He looked out at the shadows of Ravendale. 'Why did you ask me to bring you here, Mrs Royston?'

'Don't worry. I'm meeting some friends here.'

'It's very dark.'

'They'll be along in a minute.'

Hussein looked agonised. He rubbed his chin with a leathery hand. He checked his wristwatch. Then he switched off the engine ignition. 'No. I'll wait here until your friends come.'

'You'll do nothing of the sort. Your wife is set to

give birth to your baby and you should be there. So off you go.'

'I can't leave you here, Mrs Royston!'

Mrs Royston looked up and down the street. There under a streetlamp by the children's playground a few young people in hoods and baseball caps were congregated. 'Ah! Here they are now! That was lucky! Okay, you can go now, Hussein! Give my love to Sajida! Hurry! Drive carefully! Bye! Bye!'

Hussein looked back over his shoulder at the indistinct group huddled under the lamp post. He looked doubtful, but was unable to resist Mrs Royston's send-off. He started the engine up again and muttered his disapproval of Mrs Royston, himself and the world in general. Finally Mrs Royston watched him drive off. When she turned back, the three dogs were sniffing the wind. They were turned towards the small knot of young men under the lamp post. Sasha growled, low and throaty.

'Calm down, Sasha. They're no bother to us. Now then, let's see how to get into this wretched house.'

It was painful for Mrs Royston to hobble any distance. But when she saw that the house was boarded at the door and windows she was able to drag herself to the rear. It only took one circuit of the house to see where Sophie and James would have got in. But it also told her that she had no hope of clambering up there herself.

And yet she had to get in there fast. 'We're in trouble, Sasha,' she said. 'We're in a spot.'

Sasha looked up at her. Mrs Finny made a low moan, like a yelp. Tara leapt forward and licked Mrs Royston's hand.

'Don't worry, girls. Let's see who's around.'

Mrs Royston led the dogs back to the front of the house. She looked up the street to where the small knot of people were gathered earlier. They had already split up and one of the figures was heading towards her. Mrs Royston waited.

The young man moving towards her wore a base-ball cap and dirty jeans. The collar of his dark fleece was turned up as if he wanted to hide his face. He was smoking a cigarette, which he held pinched between his finger and thumb and cupped in the palm of his hand. He saw the dogs and made to give them a wide berth.

'Young man. Young man.'

He stopped dead in his tracks, looked at Mrs Royston and then glanced shiftily back up the road, as if someone might be following him.

'I need your assistance.'

'What?'

'I said I need some help.'

He looked up and down the street again, as if the police might suddenly appear. Now that Mrs Royston could get a good look at him she could see that he had terrible skin and that his eyes were like the slits of a burrowing mole. 'What?'

The three dogs had gone quiet. They all sat back, their jaws turned up towards the man. Watching him.

'I want you to help us to get inside that house.'

The man looked at the house and looked at Mrs Royston. Then he took a drag on his cigarette. 'You must be jokin', you daft old bitch.'

But Mrs Royston wasn't joking and she wasn't daft. She knew perfectly well that the man was one of the junkies who hung around the children's playground at night. She took her purse out of her pocket and counted out some notes right in front of him.

'Fifty pounds if you can get us inside.'

The man looked at the money coolly. He glanced up and down the street again. 'What's to stop me just taking the fifty pounds off you?'

'Well, you could try. But then again Sasha here would take your fingers off before you got one step. And after that, even if you did manage to get close to me, Mrs Finny here would rip your throat out. As for Tara, now she's the really vicious one, and I've trained her up to go for a man's private parts.'

The man's free hand instinctively went down to protect his 'private parts'. He grinned, and his smile was like a slash in a Halloween pumpkin. 'No need for that, I was only jokin'! Give us the fifty sobs and I'll get you in.'

'Get me in first and then you'll have your fifty.'

He sighed. Tossing his cigarette to the ground, he stamped it out with his foot. 'Hang on here for a minute.'

The man walked back the way he came. Mrs Royston watched him. Before he turned the corner out of sight she saw him rummaging in some bushes. He came back carrying an aluminium ladder on his shoulder, whistling, like a window-cleaner.

'Splendid,' said Mrs Royston. 'You look like you're used to breaking into houses.'

He gave her an old-fashioned look. 'You want me to get you in or not?'

'Let's go. Come on, girls.'

They walked to the back of the house and the man leaned the ladder against the wall so that it rested lightly on the sill of the open window. He stepped back and held out his hand for payment. 'Job done. Fifty quid.'

'Not so fast. I said get *us* in. That means Sasha, Mrs Finny and Tara here, too.'

'I don't like dogs.'

'Perhaps. And perhaps they don't like you. But fifty pounds says you'll do it anyway.'

And so they climbed in. Mrs Royston went first. When she got to the window she found it a painful struggle to drop down onto the landing inside. The arthritis in her knees made her bones jar and she was winded and out of breath. But luckily the drop was only a few feet, and by the time she had recovered, the man appeared again at the window, sweating heavily, carrying Sasha in his arms. Sasha looked like she wasn't enjoying the ride and once on the sill she quickly scrambled out of his arms and leapt down onto the landing, to where Mrs Royston stood with her torch. Sasha sniffed at the air and let out a low whine.

'This one stinks,' the man said when he appeared with Mrs Finny.

'You're not exactly what I'd describe as fragrant yourself, young man. Pass her down to me.'

When she scrambled down to the landing, Mrs Finny's ears were pricked. She seemed to want to venture deeper into the house but Mrs Royston called her to heel.

'And this one won't keep still.' Tara was also

quick to leap out of the man's arms. 'That's it,' he said, leaning over the sill reaching down for the money. 'I've kept my side of the bargain. You keep yours.'

Mrs Royston handed him the fifty pounds. 'I suppose you'll spend it on drugs,' she sniffed.

He stuffed the money straight into his pocket. 'Do I ask you what you're doing? No. So you don't ask me. Now I'm out of 'ere.'

The man's feet could be heard clanking rung by rung down the aluminium ladder. Then there was a scraping sound and finally, silence.

'You hear that, girls? The wretched man has taken his ladder. Never mind. Come on. Let's find Sophie and James.'

The dogs needed no encouragement. They dragged at their leads, but they were all behaving oddly. Their hackles were up. Tara in particular had a sinewy ridge down her back, prominent and bristling when she sensed a threat, and right now it was quivering on her like a separate, live thing. Mrs Finny was baring her teeth and sneezing. Sasha was half growling, half whining. Whatever was in the house, the dogs didn't like it. But they led Mrs Royston down the steps in the darkness, the torch beam jiggling as the dogs strained on their leashes.

Letting the dogs lead her, Mrs Royston followed

them to the back of the house, where they stumbled into a room. There she saw extraordinary things. A mattress in the corner of the room had burst into flames that were eighteen inches high. It smoked out the room but it also gave light enough for her to see Sophie and James, standing against the wall and staring at some spot in the centre of the room.

The dogs were already crazed, barking, yelping, twisting on their leads, snapping at the air, or at something Mrs Royston couldn't see.

'Mrs Royston!' Sophie shouted.

Mrs Royston could no longer hang onto the dogs. They were too strong and too determined. Dragging their leads, they all ran at the same spot in the room, biting at the air, baring their teeth. Then something flung Sasha against the wall and she howled. Mrs Finny too was flung backwards with a yelp. Tara stood firm, snapping, moving her head from side to side as if looking for an opportunity to strike. Then she too was lifted off her feet and flung against the wall.

But the dogs were back again, undeterred. They were circling, snapping and circling.

'What's happening?' Mrs Royston shouted.

'They're attacking the Gozard! You can't see him, but he's wary of them.'

It was true. Both James and Sophie could see what

Mrs Royston, despite her own powers as a *savant*, couldn't. Even though the dogs' fierce jaws were snapping at the Gozard and connecting only with thin air, the Gozard seemed unable to deal with all three at once. The drooling dogs couldn't sink their teeth into him, but they had unbalanced him. He swept them away with a gesture, yet even though he slammed them against the wall as he had done with James, they returned to harry him.

Mrs Royston hobbled across to Sophie and James. 'The *Index*! It said it's not a Gozard at all. It's something much worse. You can't fight him. We should get out of here.'

'No,' James said. 'I know what has to be done. Sophie, you've got to let Lydia come through you. She's here. It's you she needs, Sophie. It was you after all that she called to help her. You've got to let her fight him through you.'

'But how?' said Sophie. 'How?'

The dogs were tiring. They were being flung against the wall time after time, and they were yelping and limping from their wounds. Mrs Finny was already bleeding from the mouth. They couldn't possibly keep up their attack. It was only a matter of time before they limped out of the fight.

'You have to go to that *corridor* where the shimmers come from,' James said. 'You have to find a

223

way. That's the place where Lydia is. We can't beat him here, Sophie. We have to take him on in the corridor because that's where we're strong!'

Sophie nodded. She understood.

She stepped towards the Gozard as he flung Tara away from him. Mrs Finny was already beaten and Sasha was whining, ready to make a last attack on the creature, but now she too was bleeding from her nose and mouth.

Sophie took another step towards the demon. Seeing her move in, Sasha hung back with the other dogs, watching.

The demon lifted back his head, watching her come towards him. He offered her a vicious smile. Smoke was drifting from his mouth. He let her get within three steps before throwing back his head, opening his mouth and releasing in her direction a foul, poisonous blast of wind. It blasted back Sophie's hair as if she were in a hurricane. It was almost strong enough to knock her off her feet.

And a voice came to Sophie. It was the voice of William, her judo instructor. It simply said *Relax! Relax!* She looked back at the lizard eyes of the demon and his open mouth, exhaling this foul, high wind between the sharpened points of his teeth, and she relaxed her body and allowed herself to become soft, to become shapeless, to become boneless.

And as she did so she knew that she had gone into the world of the shimmers, the corridor between waking and dreaming, the halfway plane of being which had sent her the hawker and every other messenger. It was a space of white, grey and golden light. She was not alone there. The demon was there, too, looking astonished now that she had dragged him with her to this place. He looked different. He was reduced, smaller, glowing with a strange black light that was more like the dirty smoke given off by a burning tyre.

And there too was James, standing right behind her, looking not like James in the normal world but distorted, taller, more light than physical body, and he was standing right behind her. There was a fourth person in that place, too. 'Lydia,' Sophie said, or thought she said, since the word came from her mouth a long time after her mouth had moved to shape the name.

And Lydia was a beautiful hawk in that place, a hawk that seemed to come from inside Sophie and to fill the space. Sophie simply made her body available to the hawk; she became the hawk. Her claws were golden and terrifying and her eye glittered and her beak was sharp as a scythe. As a giant hawk Sophie took to the air, turned and swooped back on the demon. With a terrifying shriek the hawk swooped into the demon, tearing at his chest with her beak, grabbing at his bowels with her claws.

The demon was torn, shredded. This time, in the Corridor the demon was unable to let the attack pass through him as before. Instead his awful shriek terrorised their ears as the demon folded on his own wounds, smoke and cockroaches spilling out of him instead of guts.

And three silver arrowheads of light appeared at the wall of the Corridor, passing through, and now the three chevrons of light attacked the demon, ripping at it, shredding the shrieking monster as it spilled a growing mass of cockroaches and a rising fog of thick smoke.

'It's the dogs,' said James. 'They are spirits of light! They can come into the Corridor!'

And now even Mrs Royston could see what was happening, for she had torn off her dark glasses, and though there was a roaring in her ears and a painful flickering of coloured lights at the corner of her eyes, she too could see the Corridor of white and golden light; and she could see the glittering hawk with its sharp beak and claws that was Sophie; and James too with his sword of flame in his hand; and the three arrowheads of light that fell upon the Gozard.

And as she watched all this, the dogs ate the screaming demon.

17

The following morning Sophie stationed herself on the corner of Parkland Drive, waiting for James. The weather had turned warmer, fresh and clear; the kind of day when walking to school was a pleasure and not a chore. After a few minutes, James appeared. He was back to his old habit of sticking his nose in a book while he walked along the street. But when he drew abreast of Sophie he stuffed the book in his rucksack.

'All okay?' he asked.

'All okay,' said Sophie.

'No dreams? No shimmers?'

'No nothing. I slept like a baby.'

'Me too. Except the dogs woke me up, prowling around the room at about five o'clock in the morning.'

When they'd left Ravendale the night before, James had agreed to spend the night on a camp bed at Mrs Royston's house. Sophie of course had her family to return to, but even though they were all confident that the nightmare was over, neither James nor Mrs Royston felt much like being on their own for the rest of the night.

To get out of the house, Mrs Royston had told James where he might find a ladder hidden in the bushes near the children's playground. He'd climbed out of the house and within a few minutes he was back with the ladder. It was a struggle, but Sophie and James had managed to get Mrs Royston out of the house, followed by the dogs. Then Mrs Royston had called a cab to take them all home.

Sophie had had to sneak back into her home while her mum and dad slept. Unfortunately for her a squeaky board on the stairs had woken her dad. She heard him getting up. Sophie flushed the toilet to make out she'd been using the bathroom. They passed quickly on the landing, and her dad was so sleepy he barely noticed her.

Until breakfast time. 'Were you up in the night, Sophie?'

'Yes. Had to go to the toilet.'

Her dad rubbed his jaw and screwed up his face. 'I have this vague picture of you fully dressed on the landing.'

'Dad, you're such a drip,' Sophie said, pretending

to be more interested in spreading marmalade on her toast.

'He is, isn't he?' Sophie's mum had said.

James and Sophie walked to school in silence. 'Did you get away with coming in so late?' James said.

'Just about. How was it sleeping round at Mrs Royston's?'

'She gave me this camp bed to sleep on. Last time it was unfolded was in the African jungle in 1959. I was a bit wary of the dogs after what I'd seen them do to a demon. And let me say they kept making some pretty nasty smells.'

'Don't even go there,' said Sophie.

'No. But anyway, I feel great.'

'Me too. We're going to have to ask Mrs Royston a few questions, aren't we? Like how she knew to come after us?'

'Yes. We talked a bit about that. She said she would tell us everything over a cup of tea.'

By this time they were approaching the footbridge over the washbrook. There was a solitary figure standing in the middle of the bridge, as if waiting for someone.

'It's Suki,' Sophie said. 'I wonder if she's waiting for me.'

As they approached the bridge Suki looked up, a

little shyly. 'Morning, Sophie. Morning, James.'

James blinked. He didn't seem to be the Geek any more.

'Morning!' Sophie said brightly. 'Who you waiting for?'

'You, actually.'

'Really?'

'Yes, really.' Then Suki covered her face with her hands, before blurting, 'Look, Sophie, I think I know what you did for me. I don't know how you did it exactly, but I just know you did something – both of you. I'd been feeling terrible for weeks and weeks before that night. Then it was as if something lifted. All I know is I've been a cow to you, and I know you helped me in some way that I don't understand.'

Sophie and James exchanged a look. 'It's never going to be easy to explain,' Sophie said.

'It's okay,' Suki said. 'Maybe one day you'll feel able to try.'

'Maybe one day.'

'That's good enough for me,' Suki said. 'Now, can I walk with you both to school again in the mornings?'

'Gladly,' said Sophie.

The girls linked arms. Suki then offered her free arm to James. 'Is that okay with you, James?'

'It is okay,' James said, 'so long as we don't have to link arms.'

On the way back from school that day, James told Sophie he had something to show her; something he'd put together in Design-tech lessons that day. He made her wait until they'd found their usual bench at the church. They sat down and he took something out of his schoolbag and handed it to her.

It was a neat, grey business card with an electric blue stripe. It read:

Maslama-Picator psychic detective agency
Help is available.
SM & JP

'What do you think?' James asked.

'It's very nicely designed.'

'I thought we could put our phone numbers on it. Then I had my doubts about that. I thought I would check with you first.'

Sophie wasn't sure about that. They hadn't even discussed any kind of agency, let alone phone numbers and going public.

'You don't like it, do you?' James said, disappointed.

'Look, it's not that I don't like it. But don't you

think it's a bit soon? I mean, we don't know that we can help anyone or anything yet, do we?'

James took back the card. 'I suppose you're right. I had this idea we could help people who were in trouble. Like Suki.'

'You wouldn't be scared? Of going through something like that all over again?'

'Of course I'd be scared. Who wouldn't? But the fact is you and I have this ability and I don't think it's going to go away. Are we going to ignore it for the rest of our lives? Or use it?'

It was a good question. But even if it was a good question, Sophie's intuition told her it was more than that. A partnership between her and James, even if it was this odd idea of a psychic detective agency, was also a way of cementing their friendship. How could she possibly say no to him? 'I think it could be a good thing, James, and maybe we can do it. But if we had some cards printed, I've no idea who we'd give them to.'

James recovered his enthusiasm. 'I've thought of that. We'd give them to Mrs Royston and a very few other people who understand what we're talking about. We could keep our real names and our phone numbers out of it, and then people who were genuine would contact us by a third party, like Mrs Royston, who could keep the idiots away!'

'You have been busy, haven't you?'

'Been thinking about it all day. There's another thing. I hadn't noticed it before.'

'What's that?'

'Maslama and Picator. The initials correspond with our own initials. M and P.'

Sophie grabbed the card from James, as if to check what she'd just been told, though knowing instantly that it must be true. She turned the cards over, as if there might be something written on the back of it to help her fathom this mystery. But of course there was nothing. This was not a dream. The gravestone was just a few feet away from her, reminding her that Lydia was finally at rest, and that her friend Suki had been rescued from an evil place.

She leaned back on the bench and fixed her eyes on the church steeple pricking at the blue sky. 'Let's go ahead and have some cards printed,' she said.